DIGITAL MAGIC

MAGGIE ALABASTER

"THIS IS IT," I said.

Some people think when you get told you've been admitted to a magical academy, an owl drops off a letter to your door. Or maybe a giant tracks you down to inform you of some latent magic ability.

Of course, that only happens in fiction. In reality, they tell you by text message.

"Well, what are you waiting for? Read it." That was my best friend, Jess, her eager brown eyes a stark contrast to her bleached blonde hair.

"What if I don't get in anywhere?" I asked. My heart raced so hard I was sure the whole coffee shop heard it. I tapped on my phone screen with my fingernail.

"You won't know if you don't look," she reasoned.

"If you don't, I'm going to look for you." She made to grab the device from me.

I moved it out of her reach. "Hey, no you won't!" She would do it too, but I needed to see for myself first. "Fine, I'll look."

I waited another minute or two, took a deep breath and tapped the home button. The screen lit up. I selected "messages" and opened the text.

It read:

Ms Peyton Jane Chapel,

We are delighted to inform you of your acceptance to the Academy of Modern Magic.

Semester 1 commences on March 13.

Regards,

AMM administration.

My heart sank.

"You didn't get in?" Jess asked. "I'm so sorry. At least you can come to school with me."

I showed her my phone.

"Oh." She frowned. "Is that bad?"

"Well—"

I had wanted to attend the University of Arcana, or even the College of Advanced Magical Education. The Academy of Modern Magic was a fine school, but the others had offered education in all things paranormal for over five hundred years. In the paranormal community, as with most things in the world, prestige was everything.

Unlike the rest of the world, you can't apply to a magical tertiary institution. They choose the witch, wizard or shifter and their decision is final. Take it or leave it.

"Leaving it," meant going to a human university and learning ordinary subjects.

"It's not my first choice," I admitted. I put my phone down on the table and picked up my tea for a sip.

"But it's still a paranormal university." I didn't miss the note of envy in her tone. It jerked me out of my self-pity. In spite of being born into a magical family, Jess hadn't inherited a drop of ability. Nor was she a shifter. As paranormals went, she was normal.

"I'm sorry, I shouldn't be an ungrateful ass," I said.

"Yes, at least be a *grateful* ass," she replied.

I snorted a laugh. "I haven't decided to go yet. I could still study accounting."

"Pfft." She waved a hand and almost smacked her enormous costume jewellery ring on the table. "You would be bored out of your fucking mind. You're going to accept, you know you are. You're the daughter of the great Lucinda Knight-Chapel."

"All the more reason *not* to go," I grumbled. My mother was a prodigy. The first witch to graduate from the University of Arcana at the tender age of fifteen. Having grown up amidst adults who admired and feared her, she had never wanted, nor related to, her only child. I was an apology to my father for her always being so busy and rarely spending two consecutive nights under the same roof.

Jess shook her head and grinned.

"What?" I asked.

"I can't imagine you as an accountant, but if you go that way, can you do my taxes?"

"Fuck off," I said. I swatted her on the arm, then forced myself to be serious, at least for a while. "You really think I should accept, don't you?" I asked. This was the rest of my life we were talking about. My future in the human world, or the paranormal one. If I chose the human world, I would have to hide my ability to use magic. That would make tax time so much more tedious.

Jess put a hand over mine. "Peyton, I would have loved to go to university with you. We could have skipped lectures and gotten blind drunk together, talked about the guys and girls we screwed, and all that stuff. The truth is, I don't have your ability."

She raised a finger before I could respond. "I'm okay with that, I swear. I've had to deal with it for eighteen years. For a long time I wished I'd inherited my parent's magic, but it is what it is. Meanwhile, you have skills. You should learn how to use them."

She sat back and smiled. "We can always hang out on the weekends, right?"

My lips moved for a moment, but the words were hard to say. "AMA is in Sydney. It's too far to come back here to Melbourne for a weekend." I sighed with regret. "There's always text and video chat." We would probably see each other more than we did now.

"See, there you go." She nodded and picked up her coffee. "We'll be tired of each other in no time."

I laughed. "I'll never be tired of you." I would miss her terribly.

"What you going to tell Lex?" she asked.

I shrugged with one shoulder. I hadn't even thought about him until now. "I'll just tell him I'm going away to study. It's not like we're committed anyway." We were friends, fuck buddies, but that was all. He had made it clear he didn't want more and neither did I.

Jess nodded. "Imagine the hot paras you'll meet at AMA." She licked her lips. "Save one or two for me."

I was about to answer when a shadow moved past the corner of my eye. I turned to look, but nothing was there.

"What's wrong?" she asked.

I frowned and shook my head. "I thought I saw something scurry past. It was probably just an animal. I guess it moved too quickly for me to catch it."

She raised her eyebrows. "I didn't see anything." She leaned over the edge of the table. "It was probably a bird on the lookout for crumbs."

"It seemed bigger than a bird," I said slowly, then shook my head. "Maybe I imagined it. All this talk of going away has me on edge." In spite of that, I scanned the area. All I saw was people drinking their coffee and talking or staring at their phones. Nothing strange or out of place. Certainly no cats or dogs. Not even any children.

"It could be what you're drinking," Jess commented. "What self-respecting witch isn't addicted to coffee?"

I snorted at that. "Me. The stuff is terrible. Give me a good cup of tea any day." I picked up mine and sipped, but wrinkled my nose because it was too cool.

"See?" she said, "coffee still tastes good cold." She downed the rest of hers in a gulp.

"It still doesn't." I put down my mug at the same time a shadow passed on the other side of us. "Tell me you saw it that time?" I stood so fast my chair scraped on the floor underneath it.

Jess looked up at me, then down at the ground. "I didn't see anything. Maybe it's a," she lowered her voice, "magical thing."

I sat down with a plop and almost missed the chair. "It's possible," I whispered. Because whispering and looking around me wasn't suspicious behaviour *at all*.

I shook my head and sat up, as if I hadn't just been acting strangely. "I'm sure it's nothing to worry about," I said firmly.

A woman at the next table over gave me a funny look. I smiled back and did my best to seem like an innocent undergraduate on her summer vacation. Which I was… sort of.

She gave me a side-eye and looked away.

Jess choked back a laugh. "Smooth, Peyton, very smooth," she told me.

I rolled my eyes. "I try," I said. I pushed my dark hair back off my face and gave her a wry smile. "So, we were talking about hot university students?"

"Way to change the subject," she said approvingly. "You'll have to give me all the details."

"All of them?" I asked.

"Every. Juicy. One." She gave me a sly smile. "Come on, you know I'd do the same for you."

I barked a laugh, a little louder than I had intended. "No, you wouldn't. Please don't start now. I love you to bits, but I'm happy for your juicy details to remain private."

"As long as they stay juicy." She stuck her finger in her mouth and made a loud sucking noise.

I made a face. "It's like listening to my sister's sex life."

She pulled her finger out noisily. "You don't have a sister."

"Just you," I said warmly.

"Awww." She tilted her head. "I prefer you to any of mine." As the youngest of eight, Jess was lucky she wasn't the only one who couldn't do magic. Her two oldest brothers had no ability either. By the time her parents had her, they were accustomed to a mixed paranormal and non-paranormal household.

"For one thing," she added, "you're not as noisy as they are. Well, most of the time." She winked at me.

"When am I ever as noisy as seven other people?"

I asked. I held up a finger before she could answer. "Never mind, I can guess. That was one time."

She grinned. "Sure it was. I bet you scream like that every time."

"I—" The table rattled and interrupted my train of thought. "You felt that this time, didn't you?"

Her face paled. "I think everyone did."

The table rattled harder. Patrons leapt from their chairs and hurried toward the door.

The ground shifted underneath me when I stood. I put out my arm to keep my balance and grabbed my phone before it slid off onto the ground.

"We should get outside." Jess handed me my bag and swung hers onto her back.

"We're perfectly safe," I told her.

She gave me a meaningful look and headed toward the door.

I sighed and followed. She was right, of course. I could save us from a falling building with my magic, but not without people seeing it. What was the point of having magic if you couldn't save the people you care about? That didn't mean I wasn't ready if I needed to be. I wouldn't let us die to hide what I was. No one would believe magic was involved anyway, if I was careful.

As I stepped out into the sunlight, a shadow scuttled past me. At least as tall as me, and as wide, it flashed by before I made out what it was. I knew I hadn't imagined it this time; it made a breeze with its passing. The cool air would have been relief from this hot day, had it not given me chills up and down my spine.

The wind was followed closely by a snort, which I suspected only I heard. It sounded male, but I couldn't be sure. If it was and I caught him, he'd get a kick in the nuts for this. Fucking around with normals, and causing earthquakes made us paranormals look bad. Or it would if the normals knew we existed in their midst.

Jess was apparently oblivious to his passing. She had her phone out and was filming the tables still rattling inside the cafe, and the sign which swung back and forth outside the hamburger place next door. A car alarm went off nearby. She turned her phone toward it.

If any of the cafe's customers saw or heard anything but the earth tremor, they gave no sign. They huddled together in small groups, held each other and talked in low, frantic voices.

The ground stopped shaking after a minute or two, but my heart raced for much longer after that.

2

THE ACADEMY of Modern Magic building looked like most of those on the street. Grey stone, wide windows, a glass doorway. The root of a stunted tree cracked the sidewalk in front of it.

A sign on the wall beside the door read, "Academy of Modern Technology." If you google, you'll find a whole website listing classes which aren't held here, and no way to apply. All the links redirect to a school for normals. I know, because Jess and I looked before I left home.

I headed up the front steps and through the glass door. I half expected it to look like something out of a movie—moving staircases and weird creatures lurking here and there.

Instead, I stood in a normal-looking foyer, with

signs for self-defence, protective magic, shifter training and toilets. As for weird creatures, well I saw a few of those. I assumed they were shifters. To the untrained eye, they seemed like nothing more than ordinary cats, dogs and a bird or two. To someone who had grown up knowing paranormals existed, they looked like animals, but the way they stopped to look at me suggested they were something more.

"Dyson Gill," a voice shouted, "it's rude to shift in the middle of the corridor. Put some clothes on!"

I followed the trail of giggles to a guy who stood in the corridor leading to shifter training. He was naked except for the unapologetic grin on his face. He had dark hair, shaggy on the front, and abs which made my ovaries sit up and take notice. I couldn't resist letting my eyes wander a little lower to peek at his cock.

Yep, that sent my ovaries into a happy dance all of their own.

I forced my eyes up until he met my gaze. Oh shit, he'd caught me looking. Oops. My face turned red.

His grin widened until another guy stepped up to give him a poke on the shoulder. He winked at me before he turned away.

"Hey, sorry Kane." Dyson didn't sounds sorry at all. "Just trying to keep everyone entertained."

His friend—I assumed—had a redder face than I did.

"Yeah, yeah, just put that thing away, okay?" Kane waved at him.

Dyson wiggled his brows, but then shifted. Where a guy had stood, was now a shaggy dog of some kind. Gods only knew what breed he might have been.

"I'm sorry about him." Kane spoke to me before I realised he knew I was watching. "My brother was always the exhibitionist of the family."

"Oh, he's your brother," I said. In spite of the fading red in his face, I supposed there was a resemblance. They both had the same squarish jaw and blue eyes. That was where it ended though.

"Twins," Kane said wearily. "Not identical."

Dyson stuck his tongue out and panted.

"Are you a shifter too?" I asked without thinking. Some paranormals liked to keep what they were a secret. Fair enough, since normals might hunt and kill us if they knew. It never hurt to be careful.

"Yeah." Kane's face reddened again. He stuck out his hand. "Kane Gill."

"Peyton Chapel." I shook his hand.

He did a double take. "Chapel? As in—"

I sighed. "Yes, my mother is Lucinda Knight-Chapel."

He looked confused. "No, I was wondering if you're related to the footballer."

I gave him a blank look. What I knew about football would fit on a grain of rice. With room left over.

"Gavin Chapel," Kane said. His face lit up. "He's brilliant."

"Um, okay." I shrugged.

Kane's face fell. "Yeah, well, it doesn't matter." He eyed my suitcase. "You're new here?"

Dyson panted, but it sounded a lot like a laugh.

"Yes," I replied ruefully. "I'm not sure which way to go."

"Oh." Kane brightened again. "I can show you. Um, if you like."

I was starting to realise blushing was his thing. His face went pink again. I found it strangely endearing. I wasn't inexperienced in dealing with guys, but they didn't usually go red around me. They were usually—well—more like Dyson. Outgoing, obnoxious and sexy. Kane's shyness was adorable. And yes, he was sexy in his own way.

"That would be nice, thank you." I grabbed the

handle of my suitcase and gestured for him to lead on.

He licked his lips and said, "Dyson, you should probably go and get some clothes on."

Dyson shook his head and walked at Kane's heels instead.

Yep, obnoxious. I sure can pick it. All right, standing naked in a corridor full of people was probably a giveaway. I have nothing against body confidence, don't get me wrong. The gods know I'd like more of it myself, but walking around in the nude for attention, that was something else. Bold. Very bold. Admirable even. Poor Kane. I didn't envy him being shy and awkward with a brother like that.

"Have you been assigned a room?" Kane asked.

I pulled out my phone and checked the information package I'd received a couple of days ago. That was just after the conversation in which my mother had looked disapproving that I was coming here, while my father looked proud. Given that was their standard responses to everything I'd ever done, I put it out of my mind.

"I'm on the third level," I replied, "room 68." So close to sixty-nine.

The way his eyes were wide, I guessed he too was

thinking about mutual blow jobs. I knew how big Dyson was, but was Kane as big? Bigger maybe?

"Ah, we can take the elevator up, unless you prefer the stairs," Kane said. "Um, some witches prefer to levitate their cases."

I licked my lips and cleared my throat. "The lift is fine. I'm not a huge fan of stairs." Wow, I sounded lazy as fuck. Thanks mouth, for shooting off before my brain could catch up.

"Me either." Kane led the way to a bank of elevators. "The stairs are often packed with shifters practicing their running or flying. They can get...dangerous."

"I suppose it's safer for them than being outside," I said. "People would notice a bunch of animals running around."

"Yeah, I guess so." He didn't meet my eyes. Instead he pressed the upward arrow and stared at the screen which showed the elevator was on the fourth floor.

I looked down to Dyson, who stood with his tongue hanging out, the picture of canine innocence.

"Do shifters often walk around in their animal form?" I addressed the question to them both.

Kane answered. "Not usually. Dyson probably

made a bet with someone that he'd appear naked in front of the new arrivals."

"Ah." I nodded. "Does he bet often?" I eyed the shaggy shifter. He wagged his tail at me.

Before Kane could answer, the door slid open. He gestured us inside. The door closed behind us.

Dyson shifted and leaned against the elevator wall, arms crossed over his chest. My eye drank in his naked glory before I managed to look away.

He chuckled. "I only bet when I know I can win. I figured Kane here would forget, so I thought I'd invite you to the welcoming party tonight."

"Party?" I echoed like a dork. Well hells, how was I supposed to think straight when I stood in a small elevator with two hot guys, one of them naked and with a semi-hard cock? I was only human. Well, witch.

"Yes," Kane was looking anywhere but at his brother. "In the common room for level two." He glanced sideways at his brother. "You know there are cameras in here, right?"

Dyson grinned a panty-melting smile. "It's only skin, Kaney-boy."

"That doesn't mean I want to see it," Kane said uncomfortably.

His brother smirked, then turned his attention back to me. "I'll shift after you agree to come."

I swear he pronounced it cum. "Um, sure, sounds like fun."

"Great." Dyson returned to his shaggy form just before the door opened again. He trotted out ahead of us.

"I'm sorry about him," Kane muttered. "He's…"

"I'm sure he's harmless." I patted Kane's arm and felt the muscle under his shirt. He must work out.

"Mostly," Kane said.

We walked in silence until we reached room 68. Dyson padded to the room beside it and wagged his tail.

Message received, loud, clear and wet.

The door to 68 had no keyhole. I gave them a questioning look.

"You need to enter the code on your phone," Kane explained. "It'll punch the numbers in for you. Everything here works on magic from a phone or tablet." He sighed. "It's the new way of doing things, so normals don't notice."

I blinked in surprise. "We use modern technology as a conduit for magic?"

He seemed impressed I'd grasped the concept so easily. "Exactly. Some people here prefer to use tattoos and transfer their magic that way, so it's an adjustment for them." He gave me a questioning look, which I ignored. If he wanted to know if I had any ink, he'd have to find out for himself.

"So no learning to blast magic out my palms?" I asked.

"Not here, no. Trust me, your devices will do everything you need, and with normals none the wiser. Well, more or less."

"Right." Even the most clueless normal would notice if I knocked them backward, off their feet, whether I used a smartphone or my fingertips. Still, for subtle magic, this could be interesting.

I checked the info package for the room code— no, it wasn't triple six or six-nine-six-nine—and punched it in. The door clicked and Kane pushed it open.

The room was small, just two beds under the window, desks on either side and drawers and a place to hang clothes beside those.

"Looks like your roommate isn't here yet," Kane held the door so I could wheel in my suitcase.

I wrinkled my nose. I had never had to share a room. I didn't really want to do it now.

I put my things on one bed and Dyson jumped up on the other. He shifted and smiled.

"I'll share with you. We could just push the bed together and snuggle."

"Dyson!" Kane groaned and pushed the hair back off his face.

"What?" Dyson asked. He gave his brother an innocent look. "All right, you can watch."

Kane turned red and his pants tented. So that's how it was, huh? Kane got off on watching. I couldn't blame him. I was tempted to jump Dyson and let Kane watch. Then join in.

The idea made my mouth go dry. "So, um. Party later tonight?"

"Right." Dyson lay back, hands behind his head and looked very jumpable. "We'll see you there. Dress casual. Or not at all." He winked.

Now I went red.

Dyson stood and sauntered to the door. "I'll see you there then." He shifted and trotted out the door.

"I'm—" Kane started.

"Don't say you're sorry about him," I said quickly. "I doubt he's…uh…easy to contain."

Kane sighed. "He really isn't. Sometimes I wonder if maybe…"

"Maybe what?" I prompted.

"Maybe he's adopted," Kane finished. "Or I am. Then I remember we look alike."

I patted his arm again. "I feel your pain. Sometimes I wonder if I'm really related to my mother. She's an overachiever and I'm—" I sucked in a breath. "I'm not."

Kane licked his lips, took my hand and squeezed it. "Families are complicated."

"That they are," I agreed. "I'll see you at the party tonight then?"

An adorable grin lit up his face. "I wouldn't miss it."

"Great." I waited.

He looked confused, then realised he was still holding my hand. His face turned that shade I was starting to get used to. He let my hand go and stepped toward the door.

"Later."

"Yes, later," I agreed.

He hesitated on the threshold, then stepped out and let the door close behind him. With any luck, my roommate would be as nice.

3

"I'M ARIANA. You better not snore." A woman around my own age stood in the doorway, phone in one hand, handle of her suitcase in the other.

I looked up at her from where I sat on my bed. "Peyton. I don't know, I'm usually asleep at the time."

She frowned at me for a moment, pursed her lips, then burst out laughing. "I'm sorry, I guess I did sound like a bit of a dick. I had this whole speech prepared and it all went right out of my head the moment I opened the door."

She rubbed her forehead and tucked a strand of blonde hair behind her ear.

I raised an eyebrow at her. "You prepared a speech?"

She smiled awkwardly and tucked her phone into

her pocket. "I tend to overthink things. If I don't I—well—make a dick of myself. Only, I did anyway." She sighed.

I snorted and held out my hand. "Welcome to the club. And don't worry, I'm not that easily offended."

She dragged her suitcase behind her and shook my hand. "Witch or shifter?" She clapped a hand over her mouth as soon as the words left her mouth. "I'm sorry, I know it's rude to ask. See what I mean? My mouth gets me into a world of trouble." She stepped back and flopped down on her bed. Right where Dyson's naked ass had been only an hour or so earlier.

I shrugged. "It's probably a normal question to ask here. I mean, we're all one or the other. Usually."

"Usually," she asked.

I shrugged but didn't elaborate. "I'm a witch," I said for clarification.

"Oh, me too! I'm so glad we're both witches." Her eyes widened. "I mean, nothing against shifters, but..." She cupped a hand around the side of her mouth, as if there was anyone to hear, and in a whisper added, "I've never met one."

"Oh." I thought about that for a moment. "Are you sure? I mean you wouldn't know, right?"

"Well, damn." She stared at me. "I suppose not,"

she agreed. "Okay, I'm not *aware* of having met one. Have you?"

I tried hard not to think about Dyson and his cock. I failed.

"Er, um." I licked my lips. "I've met a couple of them since I arrived. They seem—nice."

"Thank the gods." She exhaled softly. "I'm sorry. I've never really had much to do with magic. I knew I could do some strange things, but until I got my text, it didn't really click, you know? I mean, who the hells assumes it's magic?"

I cocked my head. "Witches and wizards?"

She laughed. "Apart from them I mean. Normal people don't think magic is real."

"Some people do," I told her. Let's face it, people believe in all sorts of things, some more peculiar than others. Magic was certainly not the weirdest of them.

"I suppose that's true," she admitted. "But if they knew it was, they'd probably freak out."

"Same if they knew shifters were real." I thought back to that shadow I'd seen when I'd had lunch with Jess. I hadn't ruled out the presence of a shifter of some kind. If someone else had seen it... Then again, considering how rarely we had earthquakes in Australia and that hadn't rattled people—no pun intended—maybe they wouldn't care about a shifter.

Her eyes widened. "I might have freaked out a little when I found out. I mean, we have cats." She lowered her voice to a whisper. "Fuck, what if one of them was a shifter? I used to get undressed in front of them and… everything."

I suspected "everything" might involve vibrators or a sexual partner. Very awkward in front of a cat, I would imagine.

I swallowed hard. "Unless you fed them human food, they probably wouldn't stick around," I pointed out. I'm sure cat food was delicious—if you're a cat.

Her expression brightened. "I hadn't thought of that. You're right. Also I watched them all get born, so unless a shifter is kidnapping cats and taking their place, then it's probably not likely."

"Probably not," I agreed. Although, I'm sure there were shifty shifters out there. Speaking of shifters—

"Apparently there's a party on tonight, if you wanna go." I kept my tone light. No pressure. Besides, I was trying to hide how excited I was about it.

Ariana had other ideas. She let out a squeal which bordered on painful. "Shit yeah, I'd love to go! I've never been to a party with paranormals before!"

I winced. "You might want to just think of them —us—as people, not paranormals." It was hard enough to be different without being treated that way by those we had the most in common with.

Her mouth formed an O. "Right. I'm sorry. This is all so new and overwhelming." She brushed her hair off her face.

I smiled. "You're right, it is. I've been a part of the paranormal world since I was born, but I've never been to university before. And I've never formally studied magic. See, we're both new to this."

She sagged with relief. "Thank goodness for that. I was worried I'd get stuck in a room with someone who thought I was a clueless twat. Or worse."

"What's worse than a clueless twat?" I asked.

She thought for a moment. "A clueless twat who puts pineapple on pizza?"

I snorted a laugh. "I like pineapple on pizza."

She wrinkled her nose. "Heathen."

I stuck out my tongue at her. "Just don't tell me you like anchovies on yours."

"Well…" She looked toward the ceiling, but a smile played on the corners of her mouth.

I cleared my throat and declared, "I'm told I snore."

She put a hand to her mouth in mock dismay. "Oh no! Me too."

I laughed. "You can't complain if I do then."

"Oh, I still will," she said. "Or I'll do to you what I did to my sisters and tickle the heck out of you."

"Only if you want to be turned into a toad," I said dryly. I hated to be tickled.

She gasped. "You can do that? Can I do that?" She stared at her hand as if expecting it to unleash something terrible on the world.

"No," I said firmly. "Unless you're really a frog shifter." I gave her a shifty-eyed look.

"Shit, I don't think I am," she replied. "I mean, I would know if I could turn into a frog, wouldn't I?"

"Probably. You would have scared the crap out of yourself and your family by now. Unless, they're paranormals too?" They wouldn't be the first to keep vital information from their children in the hope they wouldn't possess any magic ability.

"No. Yes," she replied.

"I could be wrong, but I think it has to be one or the other of those," I remarked.

"It is, sort of," she replied. "My parents aren't paranormal, but my aunt Chrissy is a witch. She was always the bad egg of the family because of it."

I frowned. "So your parents knew and ostracised

her?" It could have been worse, they could have burnt her at the stake.

"My mother knew. She's her sister." Ariana sighed deeply. "I don't think my father knew why they didn't talk, they just didn't."

"So..." I ventured carefully, "how does she feel about you coming here? Your mother, I mean?"

Ariana pulled a face. "She... she doesn't know. She thinks I'm studying nursing."

Well shit, the girl has some balls, I had to give it to her. "I don't think you'll be learning to take temperatures or giving out medication here."

"I know," she said wryly. "I'm hoping I can work in the magical community. Maybe teach here some day, or work with paranormal children. It seemed easier to say nursing."

I nodded. Those both sounded like noble careers to me. "I have no idea what I want to do." I didn't want to follow in my mother's footsteps and work to keep knowledge of the existence of paranormals contained.

Every so often, normals would find out and all hells would break loose. She had to make sure the situation didn't get worse. Or so my father said. He always avoided the question of how she did this. For all I know, she had them killed. Or did it herself. I had no desire to either find out or kill people.

"You have lots of time to decide," she said enthusiastically. "You can try a bunch of different things and see what you like."

My mind pictured me trying Kane and Dyson and my mouth went dry. "What happens if I like them all?" I asked, my voice higher than usual.

Her mouth moved, but no answer came out. Finally, she said, "Maybe you can find a way to do them all?"

I choked on air and started to cough.

"Oh shit, are you okay?" Ariana leapt up from her bed and sat beside me. She started to pat me on the back and handed me a water bottle from the table beside my bed.

I nodded my thanks, opened the bottle and took a swig. Then another. I wished it was vodka but it helped me catch my breath.

"I'm fine," I said faintly. "Thank you."

"You're welcome." She slid away a little. "You seem worried about choosing what you want to do with the rest of your life."

"A little bit." I told her about my mother in as few words as I could.

She listened attentively and nodded. "Apparently

we both have mother issues," she said wryly. "Maybe they could get together some time, have coffee and talk about how disappointed they are in us."

"Until your mother finds out mine is a witch," I said. "Then things would get ugly."

"Very true," she said sadly. "Maybe some day people—I mean normals—and paranormals can live together and not keep secrets about what they are."

"There will always be people—normal and para-normal—who keep secrets." I capped the water bottle and placed it back on the table.

She gave me a funny little smile. "That's true too. Well, you never know I suppose."

"You never do," I agreed. "In the meantime, we have a party to get ready for."

"Ohhh, yes!" She grinned. "Will you help me to choose what to wear?"

"Of course. I think it's probably just casual though." Plus she would probably look good in anything. She was adorable and seemed genuinely sweet.

"Even casual, we should look our best, right?" She gave me a hopeful look.

To be honest, I'd never been particularly inter-ested in fashion or makeup, but it might be nice to make an effort for a change.

"Right." I had a feeling this was going to end with her making me look pretty, rather than me helping her choose an outfit.

"Great." She jumped to her feet. "Let's start with your hair."

"My hair?" I patted my head.

"Yes, you'd look amazing with it straightened. Maybe with a little colour here and there." She opened her suitcase and started to pull things out.

Colour? Well, what could go wrong?

"I'm so sorry," Ariana said for the hundredth time. "It was supposed to be a streak of blonde. I thought it would look cute."

I looked at the streak of green in my hair and tried to smile. "It *does* look cute," I said awkwardly. "It'll fade or grow out eventually anyway." I hoped. She had done it by magic, so it was anyone's guess what might happen.

"I'm sure it will," she said uncertainly.

"Maybe we should wait until we've taken some magic classes to try any more spells we found on the internet." I pulled back my hair and tied it in a ponytail. The green wasn't so obvious that way. Or so I told myself. Hey, my hair was green, I needed to console myself somehow.

"That's probably a good idea. I had no idea it would work like that." She leaned toward the mirror and smeared lipstick onto her lips. "Do you want some?"

I held up my hand. "Black lipstick isn't really my thing." I was surprised it was hers.

"I've never worn it before," she admitted. "But I figured I should try to look more badass."

That would explain the yellow dress with huge purple flowers and the ballet flats she wore.

"I have a way to go," she added.

"Hey, I think you look badass enough," I told her. "Besides, badass is a state of mind, not what you wear." Look at me, for example. I wore a pair of jeans with holes in the knees—torn, not designer holes—and a plain red t-shirt. I didn't even register on the badass-o-meter on the outside. On the inside, on the other hand, I rated much higher. Maybe…half a point or so.

I tugged down the front of my t-shirt to expose a little cleavage. That upped my rating by at least a quarter of a point. Woo-hoo, three quarters of a point. Only a bajillion to go before I'm an actual badass.

"Ready?" she asked.

"Absolutely." The idea of seeing the brothers

again made my heart do a somersault, triple backflip with an added cartwheel. It may or may not have landed on its feet. Knowing my luck, it had landed flat on its face and is now trending on the heart version of YouTube under the subject of "embarrassing but hilarious falls."

I grabbed my phone and shoved it into my back pocket. As far as I could tell, we couldn't get back into our room without one. How did shifters get into theirs then? Most couldn't do magic apart from shifting. Maybe they had ordinary old keys.

"Second floor common room," I said to myself.

"That's probably second floor and follow the noise," Ariana said with a laugh.

"Probably." I laughed too and headed toward the stairs with a few others who seemed to be headed in the same direction.

A couple of them glanced at me and smiled, but most looked as nervous as I felt. They must have placed all the first years on the third floor.

The minute we stepped out on the second, Ariana's suggestion to follow the noise seemed like an understatement. Music pounded down the corridor which was lined with students drinking, talking and making out. We had to push through to get to the common room.

That was packed already. Lights had been strung up around the room and flashed with no particular rhythm.

"You came!" Kane appear in front of me, wearing jeans, a worn t-shirt and a huge grin. My eyes bulged at the way his muscles seemed to be struggling to stay inside the fabric of his shirt.

"Here." He pressed a drink into my hand. "It's only beer," he shouted over the music.

"That's okay, I like beer," I shouted back. "This is Ariana."

He glanced at her, raised a finger and disappeared into the crowd. He returned a moment later with two more cups. He handed one to Ariana and toasted us with his.

I grinned and sipped. It wasn't very good beer, but at least it was cold.

"You need to think bigger, brother." Dyson appeared through the mass of people wearing a shirt so tight I could make out his lickable abs. In one hand he held four shot glasses. In the other he held a bottle of tequila.

Kane scowled. "I was getting to that."

"Sure you were," Dyson said. "Come on, let's step outside and get some air before piñata time."

"Piñata?" Ariana squealed. "I love piñatas!"

"Well, we better be back in time for it then." Dyson ushered us toward the door and out into the corridor.

We walked until we reached a spot where we could all sit and not have to yell to be heard. Dyson handed us each a glass and poured into them one by one.

"Shall we make a toast?" he asked.

I glanced at Kane, who looked annoyed at being overshadowed by his brother. "Maybe Kane should make it."

"Sure, why not." Dyson shrugged. "What'll we drink to, brother?"

Kane licked his lips and glanced at me. "To new friends?"

Dyson shrugged. "Good enough I suppose. And to having a good time tonight." He gave me a wink and downed his tequila.

I threw mine back and grimaced. I had drunk it before, but never by itself. It was probably an acquired taste. I felt buzzed almost immediately.

"Not bad," Dyson said. He locked his eyes on me and said, "It would be better licked off nice and slowly."

If I blushed, Kane turned twice as red. He looked as though he'd had the same thought, or at least he was thinking it now. He swallowed visibly. "Yeah, what he said," he muttered.

"I third that," Ariana agreed.

I could barely look at her, but when I did, she was looking at me with the same expression the guys had.

Oh my gods—yes, paranormals often believe in many—I might die right now. I wasn't used to being the centre of attention, especially like this. I felt as if my whole body caught alight.

I was saved from having to answer by a chant which echoed up and down the corridor.

"Piñata, piñata, piñata!"

"Come on, we don't want to miss this." Dyson tucked the bottle under his arm, grabbed my hand and pulled me to my feet.

Instead of heading back into the common room, he tugged me down the stairs to the lowest level and out a set of doors to a large courtyard. In the middle, two students were hanging a huge piñata from a pole. The piñata was shaped like a raven with a party hat at an angle on his head.

"Paranormal party planners are the best," Dyson said. He gave my hand a squeeze, apparently oblivious to the fact him holding it was making my knees weak.

"Who's first?" someone called out.

A slender woman with dark skin and hair stepped toward and took the stick she was offered. She closed her eyes, took a swing and missed.

The crowd cheered. Apparently whether or not she hit it didn't matter to those gathered.

She shrugged and handed to the stick to a tall, burly man with a hipster beard and man bun.

He swung and hit, but hardly made a dent in the piñata.

"Wouldn't it be easier to use magic?" Ariana asked.

"Of course it would," Kane agreed. "That's the point. It's more fun to take things slowly." He glanced at me again and blushed.

"Life is too short, brother." Dyson handed him the bottle and stepped forward to take the stick. He ran his hands up and down it suggestively.

The crowd wolf-whistled.

He gave me a wink and swaggered toward the piñata. With a flourish, he swung. The stick only caught the edge of the raven's tail and sent it into a spin.

Kane laughed. "Good try, *brother*."

Dyson bowed, then handed the stick to Kane. "Let's see if you can nail it first then."

Kane blushed.

So did I.

Kane's swing caught the raven's party hat and knocked it sideways, but not quite off.

Dyson clapped. "You did better than me. Nice work." He seemed sincere.

"Thanks," Kane muttered. He handed the stick to Ariana.

Almost skipping, she stepped closer to the hanging raven and waited for a few moments before she closed her eyes and swung. The stick connected with a thunk that sent the raven flying so hard I was sure it would snap the rope that tied it to the pole. It swung back and did a wild dance before it slowed to a regular swing.

The crowd cheered.

"Your turn." Ariana handed me the stick. Oh gods, I was going to miss and make a massive dick of myself, wasn't I? Oh well, what was new?

I swallowed hard and tried to ignore my racing heart. I focused on the raven and followed the rate it moved before I closed my eyes. I raised the stick and swung. When the stick connected to the piñata, it sent a jolt all the way down my arms. I winced.

Like before, the raven flew wildly, but the rope and the piñata held.

I shrugged and handed the stick over to the next person.

"Magic really would be easier," I remarked.

It took five more people before the raven burst open and sent its contents pouring down to the ground. I blinked in surprise, then snorted a laugh.

"Lube?" I asked.

"Of course," Dyson grinned. "This is a party!"

Scattered all over the ground were hundreds of tiny tubes of lubricant. Everyone hurried forward to grab them up and fill their pockets.

Dyson deliberately picked up one close to him, winked at me and pushed it into the back of his jeans.

I swallowed hard. My mind started to wander, imagining how and where he'd use that on me. His warm, slippery fingers, covered in a layer of cool lube…

"Thank the gods my dress has pockets!" Ariana's voice brought me back to the present with a jolt.

I snagged a couple of tubes, but that was all. I wasn't going to risk getting crushed by a bunch of paranormals just for lube. I tucked mine into my pocket and stepped back.

Out of the corner of my eye, I noticed someone watching me. I turned my head to look.

He had dark hair, cut shorter on the sides and longer on the top, and honey-coloured skin. Every stitch of his clothing was black. Every item fit so well it looked like a second skin. Maybe he was really a ninja or something. One of his eyebrows twitched, but that was all the movement from his entire face or body. If I hadn't seen that, I might think he was a statue. One good-looking enough to make me wet from a distance.

In spite of all of that, I frowned. Part of me felt as though I'd seen him before. The rest of me was sure I would have noticed if I had.

His eyes narrowed slightly.

I offered him a smile. It probably looked more like a grimace.

His expression unchanged, he turned away and disappeared into the crowds. Not hard when it was dark and most of the people there wore black. Still, there was something different in the way he did it.

"That was weird," I muttered.

"What was?" Ariana asked. She cocked her head at me.

"I… Nothing." I shook my head. The guy had probably been staring at my green streak. I touched my hair and grimaced.

"Okay, if you're sure." She looked worried.

"I am," I said firmly. "Let's go back upstairs, I feel like dancing."

It was Kane who took my hand this time and led me back up toward the common room. I glanced back several times but saw no sign of the strange guy. No doubt I would see him around at some point. I half hoped that would be the case, if only to ask why he had been staring and how he knew me. For some reason I couldn't put my finger on, I was sure he did.

5

"FOR THOSE OF you new to magic, it does not involve the use of sticks." The lecturer—"call me Madame Luc"—looked about a hundred years old and spoke in a thick accent, but her eyes were bright. She scanned the room slowly. Her gaze settled on each one of us, for a few seconds at least. Her eyes swished over me and she frowned slightly before moving on.

We all laughed nervously.

"Sticks, Madame Luc?" a student called out. She had dark hair, dark skin and wide eyes.

"She means magic wands," said another, a young man with a shaved head. "Right, Madame?"

"Oui," Madame Luc replied. "That is correct." She

rolled her rs. "For those of you who are not new to magic, in my class, you will not be learning how to use your hands." She gestured dismissively. "Oh, I know some will know how to use magic already, maybe better than me."

The class laughed again.

"But non! No. You will unlearn what you already know!" Her eyes narrowed as if we might challenge her.

"How do we unlearn?" someone muttered.

If Madame Luc heard, she ignored them. Instead she said, "Get out your devices."

Most of us had finished high school the year before. There, we were told to put our devices away during class, and not to touch them. This was a refreshing change.

"Some of you will already have been practicing with your devices." Madame pointed toward the green streak in my hair.

My face heated.

Ariana raised her hand slowly. "That was me, Madame, I did that."

Madame Luc stepped over to the table we were sharing and looked down her long nose at Ariana.

"Do you suppose you're in trouble for that?

Maybe you will get expelled for trying spells without permission?"

Ariana shrank back in her chair. "I… I don't know, Madame, I didn't think." She looked as though she was about to cry.

"You are not in school anymore," Madame declared loudly. "Did your magic harm anyone?"

Ariana glanced at me. "I don't think so, Madame."

I shrugged and shook my head. "I'm fine," I replied. "It'll grow out."

"There you are," Madame replied. "The rules are the same here as the laws of any country. No killing, maiming, and so forth. However, I recommend against using untried spells you find on the internet. They are like—how do you say this? Using google to be your doctor."

Ariana nodded. "Of course, Madame. I'm sorry." She glanced toward me, her expression somewhere between relieved and mortified. I didn't blame her, Madame Luc was a formidable witch.

"Open your browser," Madame said. "Not the normal browser, but Conjurer. Make sure you have version thirteen. Version twelve was—gah!" She threw up a hand. "Always with the glitches and crashing. Thank the gods they released the update recently. If you don't have that version, download it now. The academy internet is secure."

I had to search my settings to be sure I had the right browser. Oops, version eleven. I sighed. It would take the better part of an hour to download the latest one. I pressed the button and waited. Three second later, my phone pinged.

Update complete.

Holy fucking dancing goats, the net must be fast here.

"Woah," a guy said from the table beside ours. I presumed he'd found the same thing.

"Um, Madame," a student in the back said tentatively. "What if your device doesn't support the latest version?" I turned to see a guy with brown hair and a face full of freckles.

Madame Luc walked to a set of drawers beside her desk, opened it and pulled out the latest smart phone, still in a box. "Here. You come and get this."

"Well, if I'd known *that* was an option," the young man with the shaved head muttered.

A few people murmured their agreement, but as the student hurried forward, his face red, wearing what was obviously old jeans and shirt, I couldn't begrudge him a new phone.

"What is your name?" Madame asked him.

"Hamish Small," he said, speaking to his chest. He wasn't little though. He was tall, with broad shoulders.

"Monsieur Small," Madame Luc handed the phone to him with a flourish, "if you need assistance with anything here, you ask. While it is true that some of us bite, we can also help with your basic needs."

Hamish accepted the phone and nodded. "I understand. Thank you, Madame." He walked back to his table and sat.

"What was that about?" Ariana whispered.

I shrugged. "The paranormal community takes care of its own." Well, some of the time anyway. I'd be lying if I said there wasn't conflict, but when push came to shove, a free phone wasn't a big deal, nor were some new clothes.

"Now your browser is ready, yes?" Madame asked. "Open to paranormal.magic.ama.edu.au and type in "levitation." Then wait."

I did as I was asked and looked over to Ariana. She looked excited, but nervous. I got that. I was feeling the same thing. Sure, I had been around magic all my life, but that didn't mean I didn't have things to learn. I had never, for example, levitated anything.

"Your phone will ask what you want to levitate." Madame moved around the room, placing a small, wooden block in front of each of us. "In that field, you must ask it to lift this block."

I frowned. "What wording, specifically?" I asked.

"That is for you to work out," she replied.

I exchanged glances with Ariana.

"Is this how you usually do things?" she whispered loudly.

"No, I've never done this before," I admitted.

Her mouth formed an O. "How hard can it be?"

"Right," I said lightly. Magic was usually reasonably straightforward. We drew it from the world around us, specifically nature or things made from natural materials, including metal. It was easier to use if I was surrounded by trees, but a phone needed an internet connection. I had no idea how powerful magic might be when used via a device, apart from unlocking bedroom doors.

"All right, let's see." I spelled out, "lift block," and pressed the enter button. I watched the block expectantly but nothing happened.

"I guess it's not that then," Ariana said. "I'm going to try, "lift wooden block," and see if that works."

I nodded and watched her block. Nothing.

"Oops!" The student with the shaved head floated off his chair and toward the ceiling. "Don't try just "lift" and nothing else." He looked nervously upward, but a smile tugged at the corners of his mouth.

"Indeed, do not," Madame agreed. "At least, until you have better control over your magic. It's not your phone which is making things happen, it is you, *via* your phone."

There was a clue in there, I was sure of it. I thought for a moment, then put in the same words. This time, I focused on the block and pressed "enter". The block wobbled, but it lifted off the table a centimetre or two.

"Good!" Madame clapped her hands. "There, you see who is in charge here? You, not your technology. Now, do it for longer."

I tried, but I couldn't get the box to lift any higher. Ariana, on the other hand, made hers rise halfway to the ceiling. Just about everyone else in the class, including Hamish, did better than I did, but at least I wasn't a total failure. My block *had* levitated first. And I hadn't made myself fly around the room. Bonus.

I was about to put my phone away when it

pinged and a notification popped up. When I clicked on it, my phone went black.

"What the hells?" I frowned at my screen, then tapped at it.

"What's wrong?" Ariana asked.

"I think my phone just died, or got hacked, or something." I was becoming annoyed now. I could replace my phone and everything was backed up to the ubiquitous cloud, but it would take time to do it.

"Oh, that's—"

She cut off her words when my phone flickered back to life as if nothing had happened.

"That was strange." I checked my notifications but there was no sign of the one I had clicked on, not even amongst the ones I'd deleted. "Just a glitch, I suppose." Maybe version thirteen of Conjurer wasn't as smooth as Madame Luc had hoped.

"I guess so. Tech is weird sometimes," Ariana agreed.

"I will send your homework to your devices," Madame declared.

Everyone groaned. "Homework? On the first day?" someone called out.

"Homework at university?" moaned someone else.

Madame Luc smiled. "Oui. We do things a little

differently at the academy, especially since you're starting with some basic skills."

Another notification appeared on my phone. I looked carefully this time before I clicked, but it was just from Madame Luc, as she'd said.

"Homework, week 1, lift a small object with your device." I read out loud. "I can do that." I had been planning to practice that anyway.

"Easy peasy," Ariana enthused. "Maybe I'll even try something a bit heavier. Like—you."

I snorted. "You are not going to levitate me."

She pouted. "Oh come on, it could be fun."

"Great," I smiled, "then try it on someone else. Dyson might enjoy it. Or Kane." I pictured Kane, his face bright red, floating above the ground. Dyson—well, I pictured him naked and my face went hot.

Ariana gave me a sly smile. "I'm sure they'd like it if you tried them."

I swallowed. "Um, anyway…it looks like the class is finished." Anything to change the subject. Thinking about the guys was one thing, talking about them was another.

Ariana laughed softly. "Saved by the bell, hmmm?"

"Exactly," I said lightly. Of course, there weren't literally class bells here, but close enough. "And it's time for lunch. I'm starving." I swung my bag onto my back and headed for the door.

"Me too." She fell into step beside me. "I thought learning magic might be hard, but it's fun."

"You say that now," I told her. "Just wait until Madame Luc throws something harder at us."

"I assume you mean that figuratively?" Ariana asked.

"To be honest with you, I don't know," I admitted. "When it comes to magic, just about anything is possible." Including something or someone getting into my phone and doing the gods only knew what. I'd have to go through the settings and beef up my security, if that was even possible. If magic was involved, then changing the settings wouldn't do a thing. Well, except to make me feel better.

"Are you trying to scare me?" she asked. She didn't look even slightly scared, to be honest. She looked…excited.

"Would I do that?" I asked.

She grinned. "Probably not. Come on, we should hurry if we don't want to wait in line behind everyone else."

I nodded and walked faster to keep pace with her, but at the back of my mind was a niggling doubt that maybe we really should be scared. The problem was,

I didn't know what we should be scared of, or what we should keep an eye out for. I would just have to keep an eye out for anything. That totally narrowed it down. Not.

I sighed to myself and hoped the dining room had pizza. I could use a slice. Or several.

6

"SOME PEOPLE THINK combat training is a waste of time."

Lincoln Nash wasn't much older than I was, maybe mid-twenties at the most. Some of the students were probably older than him, but none had the hardened look he wore in his eyes. Whatever he'd seen or done in the past hung heavily on him. At least, I assumed that was the case. It was possible he was just a natural born asshole.

"Yes," he continued, "you can use magic, or teeth, beak or claw, but sometimes those aren't available to you. Even when they are, you need to use them to the best advantage. There are people out there who want you dead." His gaze scanned the silent class of wide-eyed first years.

"Over the next three years, you'll learn the basics of self-defence, both paranormal and otherwise. We'll start with the otherwise first. Next year you'll start on using your particular abilities and in third year you'll be honing them. By the end of that, you should be capable of surviving a test that would make the Hunger Games look like a party."

I glanced toward Ariana. Her lips were parted and she was blinking rapidly. For someone who had only recently learnt of her powers, this must be a lot to take in.

"Mr Nash," someone called out. "Do you mean that literally? Is there…a test of some kind?"

"First of all, don't call me Mr Nash. Sir is fine." The lecturer looked across the room and finally settled on the person who had asked the question—a student with short, spiky rainbow hair. "What's your name?"

"Carter. The correct pronoun is they. In case anyone was wondering." Carter shrugged.

Nash nodded. "Very well then, Carter. There wasn't going to be such a test, but there is now." His expression was completely deadpan.

A few students chuckled uneasily, while others groaned.

Carter laughed. "Good one, Mr, I mean, sir. You had everyone going for a minute there."

Nash shot Carter a look and their smile faded.

Without clarifying whether or not he was joking, Nash looked away. "Right then class, pair up and spread out."

Before I could move, Nash had grabbed my arm and pulled me aside from the group. I wasn't prepared for the jolt of lighting that passed through my arm and went straight to my groin. He frowned at me as though I had done something. Apparently he'd felt it too. He licked his lips and looked away.

Ariana looked stricken for a moment before she stepped over to pair up with Carter.

"Face your partner," Nash ordered. "You're going to try to flip each other. No shifting, no magic or there will be consequences."

I waited to hear what those were, but apparently that was all the information he was going to give for now.

"Now watch."

Before I could respond, I found myself on my back. Nash straddled my hips and pinned my hands to either side of my head.

Well hello there.

I swallowed hard.

"If I was armed, or shifted into an animal with big teeth, you would be dead right now," he told me. "Or worse."

I laughed awkwardly. "Lucky you're harmless then."

He quirked one eyebrow and the corners of his mouth tugged upward a fraction. "Never make that assumption." He climbed off me and held out his hand.

Thank the gods I didn't have a cock, or my pants would have a pretty little tent for the whole class to see. I grasped his hand and let him pull me up, but I watched for a sign he might use the opportunity to flip me. Yeah, I'd seen that move in movies plenty of times, and wasn't born yesterday.

When he made the move, I was ready. I let him pull me forward a step, then I tugged him, popped out my hip toward his groin and flipped him over my shoulder. He landed on the practice mat with a grunt.

A titter of laugher—yes, that's a thing, look it up—passed through the class. For a moment I though Nash might be angry. Instead, he looked impressed.

"You've learnt this before." He got to his feet, his hands close to his body.

I shrugged. "My parents insisted I learn to take care of myself."

He nodded. "Good, but there's still room for improvement. Maybe you should try to join the academy team. We meet on Friday after last class. No guarantees though, we only take the best."

I blinked. "Me? I..." would be wet as hells the whole time I was around him, but there were worse things in this world. "I suppose I could." Who was I kidding, he'd waved a challenge in front of me like a rag to a bull. I suspected he knew that too. There was nothing most paranormals liked more than a challenge, especially me.

He nodded. "Good. Let's try again. Everyone stop and watch—" He cocked his head at me.

"Peyton," I supplied.

"Right. Watch us and learn." He licked his lips in a predatory way that made my heart race. He was dangerous, I had zero doubts about that, but I would learn a lot from him. About self-defence, get your mind out of the gutter. Or leave it there, because that was where mine was.

"UGH, EVERYTHING HURTS," Ariana groaned. "Carter

seems nice, but they had me on my back more often than not. It's not fair to pair me up with someone stronger than me."

I frowned at her across the lunch table. I hurt too, but I didn't mind it too much. I hadn't done serious exercise in a while and it showed. I really did need to remedy that.

"If anyone tries to attack you, chances are they'll be bigger and stronger than you," I pointed out. "Or a shifter. What will you do then, stop and tell them, "My, what big teeth you have?" Because I don't think the big bad wolf is going to take the time to answer."

Ariana grinned. "I suppose not." She rolled her shoulders. "Can you teach me what you did to Nash?"

I hesitated. "I suppose so, but I'm not a black belt or anything."

She stopped mid-roll. "You're better than I am. Or anyone else in the class. You might even be better than Nash."

"I doubt that," I replied, "but thank you. Maybe we can practice before Friday. I'd hate to get there and be laughed out of the team before I even join."

"You won't," she said with more confidence than I felt. "You're amazing."

"Thank you." Dyson plopped a tray down beside mine and slipped into a seat. "I do try." He grinned.

Ariana rolled her eyes. "I wasn't talking about you, silly."

"Silly?" He put a hand to his chest in mock offence. "I'm hurt you would say such a thing."

"She's just being honest." Kane flopped down beside Ariana.

"Wow, kick a guy when he's down, why don't you?" Dyson told him.

"With pleasure." Kane bit into his burger and smiled.

"Speaking of pleasure." Dyson's eyes slid to me. "Would you like to go out tonight?"

Kane almost choked on his burger. Ariana patted his back as he coughed.

"What's up, brother? Disappointed I beat you to it?" Dyson asked him.

"I…" Kane blushed. "I was going to ask, I just…"

"Just…" Dyson prompted. "Just what?"

Kane mumbled something.

I cleared my throat. "Does anyone want my answer?"

"I do." Ariana looked curious.

I didn't know what to say to her, so I turned to

Dyson. "I would love to." Then to Kane, "Maybe we could make plans for another night?"

He nodded while still trying to catch his breath properly.

"There, see, that was easy." I sat back in my chair. Two dates, no strings. It seemed simple enough to me. At least simple as dating could ever be. If either of them thought they'd tie me down, they were mistaken. Better they know that now, before anything got too far.

"Excellent," Dyson looked pleased with himself. "After our date, you'll forget all about my brother." He shot me a wink which burned a path right down to my belly and set it alight.

"Dream on," Kane said. "I'm not that easy to forget. After our date, all you'll say is, "Dyson who?" You'll see." That last was directed at his brother.

"Perhaps you should see a vet," Dyson suggested, "you appear to be suffering from delusions." He grinned slyly.

"Fuck off," Kane growled.

I glance at Ariana and we rolled our eyes at them both.

"Men," she muttered.

"Amen to that," I replied.

Something moved past me, close enough to touch my arm lightly and send shivers down my spine.

"Who did that?" I asked.

Ariana frowned. "Who did what?"

I put my fingers to my arm. "Someone brushed past me."

"There's no one there." She glanced around, confused. "At least, I didn't see anyone."

"I didn't either," Kane said.

"Neither did I," Dyson said, "but witches and wizards can hide behind a bubble of magic."

"Yeah, I guess that was what it was," I said uncertainly. It was probably some dumbass trying to play a trick on me. It wouldn't be the first time a paranormal pranked another. "That reminds me, there was a weird guy at the party."

"Only one?" Dyson asked jokingly.

I snorted. "Okay, several, but one in particular." I told them about the starey guy who had disappeared into the crowds.

"I can think of a few people who fit that description," Dyson said slowly. "In case you hadn't noticed, paranormal academies are havens for weirdos."

"Like you." Kane smirked at him.

Dyson shrugged. "Guilty as charged. You're no

less strange than I am though. You might even be more so."

Kane stuck his tongue out at him. "Am not."

Dyson sniffed. "Apparently you're more childish."

Kane laughed. "I'm not that either."

"Anyway," I drew the word out. "This guy could be any number of guys here. I have a feeling I know him from somewhere, but I don't remember having seen him. I'll know him if I see him again though."

"You might have another admirer," Ariana suggested.

"That would be odd, for sure," I said. "I'm used to having none."

"You?" Dyson said in disbelief. "That would be like saying Kane isn't a virgin."

Kane blushed and muttered something which sounded like, "What would you know?"

"Oh, I know plenty. I even know which are your favourite videos on Porn Hustle. You like the—"

Kane flushed even more red than I'd seen him. "All right, all right, no one needs to know that."

"Oh, I don't know, these two might be curious." Dyson gestured toward Ariana and I.

I *was* curious. While I was no fan of porn made just for men to enjoy, I'd watched my share of it.

What I didn't want, was for Dyson to embarrass his poor brother any further.

"Not especially," I said lightly. "I think that's a personal thing between a guy and his electronic devices."

"Exactly," Kane muttered.

"I agree," Ariana said. Her own cheeks were an adorable shade of pink. I guess she partook as well. She'd get no judgement about that from me, that was for sure. In fact, after all this talk and my class with Nash, I might need to find some time alone with my own electronic devices. Yes, plural. You know one is my dildo, okay? I know it's not technically electronic, but you get the idea.

Dyson huffed. "Fine, I won't share his. Personally I like the ones where the guys goes down on the girl for ages and ages." As he spoke, he locked his eyes on mine. I had no doubt of his meaning. I better wash down there extra well before our date tonight. Just in case.

7

"Jeans or a dress?" I stood in front of the mirror and frowned. In one hand I held a red, low-cut tank top. In the other, I held a short, black dress. I held one in front of me, then the other.

"You'd look gorgeous in either of them." Ariana didn't even glance up at her phone when she spoke.

I lowered both. "Are you all right? I can stay here if you need me to."

She glanced up for a moment. "No, it's fine. Go and have fun." She looked back toward her phone.

I lay the clothes on my bed and sat beside her on hers. "Do you want to talk about it?"

She turned off her phone and put it aside. "I'm okay, really." Her eyes begged me to leave it alone.

I gave her a long look. "I won't push, but if you

want someone to listen, I'm here. Any time, okay? I mean, we're friends, right?"

"Right." She licked her lips and looked away.

I hesitated for a moment, then rose and grabbed the tank top and some jeans. Casual would probably be the better way to go. I slipped into the small bathroom we shared between the two of us, took a quick shower and changed.

When I stepped back into the room, she was gone.

I sighed and did my hair into a ponytail before I threw on a hint of makeup. I had only known Ariana for a handful of days, but I didn't want to think she was upset with me. It occurred to me maybe she liked Dyson or Kane and I could have kicked myself for not asking. When I saw her next, I would get that out of her. In the meantime, I would go and enjoy myself.

I tucked my phone into my pocket and slipped out to meet Dyson at the front the door to the academy.

His eyes lit up when he saw me and he licked his lips.

"Hey, sexy," he said by way of greeting.

"Hey," I replied. "You're not looking bad yourself." Not bad? He wore black jeans and a dark grey t-shirt which hugged his body in a way that made me want to tear his clothes off and fuck him right there against the wall. Hard and fast and…

Instead, I smiled. "Where are we going?"

He offered me his hand and led me out the door. "I thought we could go to somewhere beside the harbour. I know a place."

I knew a few places too, but most you had to book twelve to eighteen months in advance. Needless to say, I'd never *been* to any of these places.

"Don't believe me?" he asked teasingly. "Don't worry, I know all the best places to *eat*."

I blushed a little. "I'm sure you do. Just like I'm sure you know just the right way to play with your food."

He grinned. "I absolutely do. I'm happy to demonstrate. But after we have dinner. We might need our strength."

I swallowed. "Yes, we might just."

He led me over to an ancient VW and opened the passenger side door.

"Is this roadworthy?" I asked. The rust around the front and back of the car didn't exactly fill me with confidence.

"Of course it is," he replied easily. "Failing that, you could always ride on my back."

I eyed him and slipped into the car seat. I doubted his dog form was big enough to support my weight for more than a short time. At least he hadn't made any silly jokes about riding around on broomsticks. I couldn't think of anything worse than flying around with a stick up my butt crack. Magic didn't enable me to fly anyway, so that point was moot.

He chuckled and walked around to the driver's side. To my surprise, the car started the first time.

"My dad is a mechanic," he explained. "The rust is *just* this side of legal, but the rest of the car is fine. Trust me."

"You know the only people who say trust me are people I shouldn't trust, right?" I asked dryly.

He grinned and put his foot down. The car jolted forward, but then headed along the road at not much more than a crawl.

I burst out laughing.

"What? You expected a Maserati under the hood?" he asked.

That made me laugh harder. "Not exactly, but…"

"I know, I know." The smile never left his face. "You know what they say about guys with fast cars and small dicks. Well, you've seen my dick, so you know why my car is slow."

I considered that for a moment. "You know, I find

I can't argue with that." And now my mouth was dry, thinking about his cock and what it would feel like under my fingers.

"I mean, I don't want to brag or anything."

I shook my head. "Maybe we should change the subject." As fascinating as his dick was.

"Good idea. I love my cock, but I'd like to hear more about you."

I shrugged. "I'm pretty boring. What do you want to know?"

"Everything," he replied.

"That's not very specific," I remarked. "You might need to narrow it down, just a little bit."

"Okay, let's start with where you were born. Did you always know you were a witch? Have you met a dog shifter before?"

"That's a lot of questions. Which do you want me to answer first?"

"Start at the beginning?" he suggested.

"Fine." I leaned back into the car seat. "I was born in Melbourne. I guess I've always known, because I don't remember a time when I didn't. My parents are both paranormals—witch and wizard—so I was raised in the community with other paranormals. My earliest memory is of my father cleaning up a bowl of stew off the floor after I blasted it there."

Dyson gave a snort of amusement. "You were a bit of a brat?" he asked.

"Of course not," I replied, "I just really didn't like fish stew."

"Oh, that's unfortunate."

I glanced over to him. "Why is that? Are we going to a fish stew restaurant?

"Well…" He drew the word out. "Actually no, I'm allergic to seafood."

"That's a relief," I replied.

"And chocolate," he added.

"Really? That sucks." Although, it did mean I didn't have to share.

"Dog shifter," he said. "Apparently that also means I can't have stuff dogs can't."

"Oh, that sucks. So no wine either?"

"Nothing with grapes," he agreed. "Luckily beer and spirits are okay though. And doin' it doggy style."

I groaned. "I should have guessed you'd go there."

"Too predictable?" he asked.

"Just a little." I held my fingers slightly apart. "That leaves me with the last question. I've met a few shifters—usually friends of my parents—whose shifter form I don't know. They could have been dogs. Or birds. Or—anything."

"Insects?" he suggested. "I knew a guy who could turn into a scorpion. Nasty piece of work, he was. Him and his brothers."

"Scorpions are known for their aggression," I pointed out.

"These guys lived up to it, and then some. Still, they could have been mosquitoes or something really nasty."

I wrinkled my nose. "They'd get squashed if they came near me."

He chuckled. "Me too."

"So—have you always known you were a shifter?" I asked.

"Kind of." We stopped at a set of traffic lights and he looked over at me. "My parents are both shifters, from a long line of shifters, so they figured Kane and I would be too. They just didn't know what we'd shift into. I think they were hoping we'd be wolves, or something like that. Bears, maybe."

"They weren't happy with a big, ole shaggy dog?" I asked lightly.

"Since they're both wolves, not really. I had a dorky uncle Bob who's a dog. He's the clown of the family. Or was until I came along. I suppose they didn't want me to end up like him."

The light changed and we moved again.

"How did he end up?" I asked, hoping he didn't mind me asking.

"He's a funeral director," Dyson replied.

I blinked in surprise. "I didn't expect that. Why is that so bad?"

"It isn't, but my parents expected me to do something useful, like join the military. The academy has a recruitment program that leads directly into a paranormal unit of whatever armed forces the student prefers."

My mouth popped open. "There's a unit of witches and wizards?"

"And shifters," he said with a nod. "Depending on their performance, they can then go into a regular unit."

I shook my head, my mind blown a little. "I had no idea they knowingly let paranormals join the armed forces."

"It's a little known fact," he said, "but think about it. Do you believe World War two was won using only conventional weapons?"

"Are you saying the atomic bomb was actually magic?" My stomach turned at the idea of magic being used in that way.

"I don't know," he admitted, "but there was a

whole female unit called the Night Witches. Do you think that was a coincidence?"

"I suppose not," I agreed. "So what do you want to do when you grow up?"

He hesitated. "I want to be a kindergarten teacher. Where better to mould youngsters into open-minded adults?"

Where indeed. "That's great. The world needs more awesome teachers."

"Awww, you think I'm awesome?" he asked. "If I was my brother I'd be blushing by now.

I laughed. "I knew the academy had an education degree, but how is it different to a normal university?"

"We're taught to look for paranormals and quietly teach them to use their abilities," he explained. "And liaise with their parents. It's a big adjustment for some of them, especially those who had no idea what they were."

"I imagine it would be a shock." I thought about Ariana and what she must have felt when she'd found out.

"Exactly. Kane, being a massive geek, is studying science. He wants to know how paranormals came about and why normals can't do the things we can."

"Oh, that sounds interesting." I had often

wondered the same thing myself. Could normals become paranormal, or the other way around? The idea was oddly compelling, but not something I wanted to devote my life to exploring.

"You really think so?"

We must have reached our destination because he drew up to the side of the road and parked the car.

"I really do." I unclicked my seatbelt and opened the door. At least they had an idea of what they wanted to do. I had none. Not even a little bit. Well, except to enjoy myself tonight.

"Just between us," he offered me his arm, "don't ask him about it, unless you want to hear science stuff for hours."

I accepted his arm. "I'll bear that in mind." Although it sounded interesting to me. "It's fantastic you both have things you're passionate about."

"Something we're definitely not lacking in is passion." He gave me a wink which made my heart flip. My palms were suddenly sweaty.

"I'm sure you're not." The burst of heat in my stomach travelled through my entire body and almost made my toes curl. Part of me wanted to drag him into the back seat of his car and find out.

But first, food.

8

"How did you find this place?" I asked. The food was so good, if I ate another bite, they'd have to roll me out the door. I was pretty sure everyone here was a paranormal of some kind. It was nothing I could point to specifically, just a vibe. A hint of magic in the air, perhaps.

"I know a guy who knows a guy," Dyson replied. "Actually guy who knows a girl who knows a guy who… You get the idea."

I laughed softly and downed the last of my wine. "I get it. Don't tell me, you're really shifter royalty of some kind."

He cocked his head. "Is there such a thing? Maybe there should be. Can I just declare myself king or something?"

I pretended to think seriously about it for a moment. "I think you have to invade something first. Besides, isn't Kane the older brother? That might make him king first."

Dyson clicked his fingers. "Damn, that's a big flaw in the plan. Never fear though, I can think about an invasion and plot to overthrow my brother at the same time."

I snorted. "Should I start calling you Your Majesty?"

He waved a hand in dismissal. "Nah, but you can bend the knee any time." The look he gave me made my pulse race and sent blood throbbing through my lower body and between my legs.

"I'll bear that in mind," I said as coolly as I could, which wasn't very cool because my voice broke on the last word. Stupid voice. I swallowed and smiled sweetly, as if nothing had happened.

He gave me a knowing smile in return. "I'll pay for dinner."

"No." I sat up straight. "I will. I mean, I'll pay for mine."

"Independent girl, I like that." He nodded approvingly and pulled out his phone.

We had both had ours in our pockets until now.

A guy who didn't stare at his screen all night was a refreshing find.

We rose and tapped our phones on the machine at the front of the restaurant. Modern technology, it was like its own kind of magic.

"It's almost too easy, isn't it?" he said as we walked out into the autumn night air. "Tap, pay, forget."

"You sound like my father," I teased.

He tucked his arm into mine. "Either your father is very hip, or you're implying I sound like an old fart."

I leaned into Dyson. "I wouldn't rule out either of those things," I teased.

He chuckled. "Do you feel like a walk beside the harbour?"

No. I feel like dragging you into a dark alley, tearing off all of your clothes and licking my way up to your...

"Sure. It's a nice night out."

The sky was clear, although the city lights all but obscured the stars. The air held a hint of late summer, even though it was April. Winter never fell too hard here, but the weather would cool soon enough to dress warmly against it in a month or two.

We made small talk as we walked toward the foreshore. As always, the bustle of people and sound of restaurants echoed across the water. Sydney, like all big cities, never slept. Still, we managed to find a bench away from anyone and, if not in darkness, at least it was darker here than in other places.

"This is more like it," Dyson said as he pulled me to him. "Nothing against crowds, but sometimes it's nice to be alone." His mouth was so close he breathed warm air on my cheek and neck.

I shivered. "It is," I agreed. "What do you normally do when you're alone?" The question was so stupid I could have kicked myself for asking it.

He laughed softly and leaned in to nibble my neck. It sent a burst of heat between my thighs.

"Usually I sleep, or fantasise about beautiful women, like you," he murmured.

My face heated. "You think I'm beautiful?"

He sat back and looked at me in surprise. "Of course I do, you're gorgeous. In fact, there's nothing hotter than a woman who doesn't realise how gorgeous she is."

Before I could respond, he pressed his mouth to mine, firm, but with promise. His tongue slid across my lips. I opened my mouth to let him probe inside.

His hand went to my hip. I wanted to beg him to touch me all over, but his hand stayed there until he pulled back.

His face was flushed, but he smiled. "I should get you back before you turn back into a pumpkin."

The way his jeans tented in the front suggested he felt what I felt. The fact he was willing to step back and wait was both endearing and infuriating. My body was on fire and I wanted to be doused. On the other hand, there was no rush. It wouldn't hurt to get to know each other first.

Ok, it might hurt, but I'd live.

I nodded and let him pull me to my feet. "For the record, that's not what happened in that fairytale."

He shrugged. "I've always thought it was more plausible than wearing a shoe made of glass. Wouldn't it snap when she put her weight on it?"

"Probably," I agreed.

He laced his fingers in mine and we walked slowly back to toward the car.

Before we got more than a few dozen footsteps, something rushed past me.

I froze.

Dyson stopped and turned back to me. "What is it? Is something wrong?"

"You didn't feel that?" I scanned around in front of me and listened.

"I feel a lot of things right now," he said jokingly, "you might need to be more specific."

I huffed a laugh. "It felt like something brushed past my leg."

He frowned. "I didn't—"

Something whizzed around both of us, fast enough to whip up a breeze. It paused and for a split second I caught sight of—

"That couldn't possibly be—"

"I think it is."

Then it was gone as fast as it had come. I waited for a long time, but if it came back, it concealed itself better. After maybe five minutes I almost was sure it was gone. Only then did I sag slightly.

"Either I'm losing my mind, or that was a gargoyle," I said.

"If you're losing your mind, then so am I," Dyson agreed. "I've heard about some…weird shifters, but I've never seen one before."

"You think that was a shifter?" I asked.

He shrugged. "What else? Gargoyles aren't usually a thing, unless they're carved out of stone."

"Gargoyle shifters aren't usually a thing either," I said softly. I frowned. "Wait, what do you mean you've heard of some weird shifters before?"

"Just that," he replied. "Most shifters are animals of some kind. Occasionally they're animals which are now extinct, but… I've heard some can shift into creatures that never existed."

"Like gargoyles."

"Exactly. And—believe it or not—dragons." He ran a hand over his hair and looked troubled.

"Dragons?" I echoed. "How?"

"I'm not sure. A combination of magic and the ability to shift. But—not, because they don't exist."

I had already guessed magic was involved in some way. I hadn't seen the gargoyle because they had been inside a bubble of magic. The ability to make oneself invisible was a basic skill for most witches and wizards, although it was often the bane of their parents. Luckily sound escaped the bubble, so giggles helped to locate wayward young paranormals.

The gargoyle had dropped their bubble for long enough to show us what he was, if not who. The question was why? Well, that was one of the questions anyway. I asked Dyson another, "Why the hells is a gargoyle following me around?"

He raised his hand in a shrug. "Because he thinks you're cute too?"

I rolled my eyes slightly. "What makes you think they're a he?"

"Just a vibe I got," Dyson replied easily.

"Oh, for a moment there I assumed gargoyles could only be male." I quirked an eyebrow at him.

"Non-existent creatures, just like regular para-normals, can do or be whatever they want," he said easily. "They won't get any judgment from me."

"Me either."

He nodded. "I had a feeling you wouldn't. You don't seem the type to go around judging people."

"My life is complicated enough," I replied. "Is it true that trans shifters can shift into the sex they feel best represents them?"

He swung our hands between us and started to walk again. "It is. A trans woman shifter can become a lioness. Cool, huh?"

"Very," I agreed. "I guess magic gets it better than the outside anatomy does."

"Magic is as clever as fuck," Dyson agreed. "Smarter than me, even."

I laughed. "You're so modest."

"Not in the slightest," he said unapologetically. "Why try to hide it when you're good looking, talented, clever…"

I shook my head at him. On anyone else, his brash nature might be annoying. On him, it fit like a tailored suit and expensive shoes. Or board shorts and bare feet.

"Seriously though, should I be worried if a shifter slash witch or wizard is following me?" The question was mostly rhetorical. Given my mother was a powerful witch, she had enemies. There was always a chance that sooner or later she'd piss someone off enough that they'd come after me. If that's what this was, the sooner we got back to the academy, the better.

"I think between us we can take care of any magic slash animal they throw at us," Dyson replied. "I heard about your skill in self-defence. Maybe you could give me some pointers some time."

"I'd be happy to," I said, although I don't know what I could teach a guy who could shift into an animal which could rip a person's throat out if he wanted to. I guess he might not always be in a position where he could shift. It never hurt to be too careful.

Without giving him any warning, I had one arm twisted behind his back and the other pressed to the wall beside him. He was taller than me, tall enough that my eyes were level with his chin. His mouth opened in surprise.

"Lesson number one, always be on guard against attacks," I told him.

"Um, I'll bear that in mind." He leaned down to kiss me but winced at the pressure on his arm.

"Oops, sorry." I let him go and took a step back.

He rubbed his arm lightly. "Remind me not to piss you off."

I smiled wryly. "I really didn't mean to hurt you."

"If anyone asks, I'll say I fell over my own two feet." He took my hand again.

"Rather than say a woman got the better of you?" I asked, a little more touchy than I intended.

"Absolutely not!" he replied immediately. "Rather than admit I was caught off guard. I have a reputation to uphold, after all."

"Oh, you do?" I asked.

"Of course. Who ever heard of a dog being caught unawares?"

I had no answer for that. "Why is Kane so shy about saying what he can shift into? Is it really that bad?"

"That depends what you call bad," Dyson said. "I'm not telling you though. That would violate the bro code."

"Bro code?" I laughed.

"Yes. Even though we fight, and he thinks I'm a dick, there's still things I wouldn't do. Lines I wouldn't cross."

"Dating the same woman is all right?" I asked tentatively. Plenty of guys wouldn't be okay with it.

"As long as everyone is consenting, then anything goes," he replied.

I nodded. "So tell me, is walking around naked in the corridors something you do often?"

He threw back his head and laughed. "Not usually, but I made a bet. I couldn't very well lose, could I now?"

"I guess not." It's not the kind of bet I would make made, but each to their own. "What would you have lost if you had?"

"Ah now, that would be telling." He tapped his nose with his finger.

"Don't tell me, bro code?" I asked.

"Something like that," he agreed.

We reached the car and he opened my door before walking around to the driver's side.

I stopped with my hand on the door and looked around. I had that feeling again—that someone was watching. Could it be the gargoyle shifter? How did a gargoyle shifter even exist? I would say something about it all was off, but the whole thing gave me the chills. Whatever I did, I would have to watch my back.

I slid into the seat and closed the door firmly

behind me. The clunk it made was satisfying. They just don't make cars like they used to.

I resisted the urge to lock it. If the gargoyle wanted me dead, I probably would be. Showing himself to us was a warning, I was sure of it.

What I didn't know was why.

9

"PEYTON, can I talk to you after practice?" Nash's expression was as intense as ever, but there was something more today. Something I couldn't quite read.

Curious, I nodded, "Sure, sir." I was slick with sweat after a rigorous training session, but I felt good. Since joining the academy's combat team, I was more fit than I had ever been. Nash rarely smiled and pushed us all to the edge of our limits, but he kept us on our toes. We all bitched and complained about aching muscles and all the hard work, but by the end of a session, I knew he'd wrung more out of me than I'd known I'd had. By the end of the first month at the academy, I'd even dropped a dress size.

I'd spent much of that month keeping an eye out for the gargoyle, or some other mythical creature, but saw nothing out of the ordinary. After a few weeks, I started to forget about it. Maybe whatever it was about wasn't going to happen after all.

I grabbed a towel and wiped my face. What I needed right now was a cold shower. Being around Nash, Dyson and Kane, but with nothing happening with any guy, I was getting antsy. Sharing a room made it all the more perilous. A girl could only have so many "extra long" showers before it became obvious as to what I was doing in there. Not that I was ashamed of masturbating, but I would always feel uncomfortable doing it when Ariana was sitting in the next room listening to the water flow.

I flopped down onto the mat and stretched while everyone filtered out of the training room. It wouldn't do to have sore muscles tomorrow. Saturday was party night, when a bunch of us would head to the city and drink and dance until the sun came up. Waddling to the train with stiff muscles would be embarrassing, to say the least.

Finally, Nash sat beside me and wiped his face with his own towel. "You're doing well," he said simply.

"Thanks." Gods, he might not be the friendliest

guy, and he was a teacher, but damn, having him sit so close made my heart race.

He nodded. "I was wondering if you wanted to do some extra training? One on one?"

I almost choked on my pent up lust. *One on one? Oh hells yeah.*

"Um," I squeaked. For real, I squeaked. "I, uh—" Have lost the ability to be articulate. *Fuck.*

"You don't have to," he said, a slight frown on his brow. "I just thought—you could be amazing?"

"I'm not already?" The stupid words left my lips before I could stop them.

He smiled—actually smiled—although it was faint. "As a matter of fact, you are, but there's always room for improvement."

I blushed. "Yeah, that's true. The bit about improvement, I mean. I've learnt a lot from you already but I'm sure I can learn more." Some of it might actually be related to hand to hand combat.

"That goes both ways." His expression gave away nothing. "You're never too old to learn."

I snorted softly. "You're not old at all."

He ran a hand over his head. "No, I suppose not. Sometimes it feels like—" He shook his head. "It doesn't matter."

"No, it does." I put a hand on his arm. "If you want to talk about it, I'm a good listener."

He licked his lips. "Let's just say it's been a long road to get here. I won't bore you with the details."

"I bet they aren't boring," I assured him.

He thought about that for a moment. "No, you're right, they're not, but there's a lot I'm not proud of."

"No one's perfect." I lowered my hand to the mat. "Not even me."

"Are you sure about that?" The corners of his eyes crinkled.

"Are you teasing me?" I asked.

"Maybe just a bit," he admitted. "Why, does it seem like the stick is so far up my ass I can't make a little joke?"

"Well—" I hedged.

He sighed. "Like I said, there's a lot I'm not proud of."

"Did you kill anyone?" I intended it as a joke, but the laughter died before it left my throat. His face was like a stone wall, except the sides of his mouth, which were pulled back so hard I thought he might snap.

The blood drained from my face. "You did?" I should probably get up now, run away and never look back.

"To be clear," he said, his voice as tight as his expression, "I only did it because they would have killed me first if I hadn't. And some friends—well, allies—also."

I licked my lips. "Is that why you're here? Because of what happened?"

"In a manner of speaking, yes," he replied. "To keep them safe, to keep myself safe and to teach paranormals like you to do the same." His eyes searched my face as though he was looking for something behind my eyes.

"I understand," I said softly. "Sometimes life makes us do things we don't want to do. People get hurt, or worse. As long as you don't go around looking for trouble…"

"At times, trouble finds us," he said, "but if I could have avoided taking a life, I would have."

I nodded. "I believe you."

For some reason, he looked relieved. He nodded. "Good. You're the first person I've told." His expression turned anxious. "You have to swear not to breathe a word to anyone."

"I swear. Who would I tell anyway?" I asked lightly.

He raised an eyebrow at me. Okay, he was right, I had a few friends I could blab to, but I wouldn't.

"I mean it, I won't tell anyone," I assured him. I held up a finger. "I pinky swear."

He looked taken aback but hooked his finger around mine and we shook.

The next thing I knew, he'd pulled me to him and mashed his lips against mine. I was so shocked I couldn't breathe for a moment. Then I was kissing him back. My tongue tangled with his and my arms wound around his neck.

My heart racing, I lay back and pulled him down with me, so he lay over me, his mouth on mine.

If he was surprised by this turn of events, he gave no sign. He didn't even pause. Instead, he took my hands, pinned them above my head and straddled my body. I wound my legs around his hips and ground myself against his growing erection.

He groaned. He kept one hand on my wrists and the other ran down my sides to cup my ass. By the time he slid it around to rub at the front of my leggings, I was all but panting. I rubbed myself against his hand, wanting more, needing more.

He pulled at the front of my leggings and slipped his hand inside and under my panties.

"Oh, gods," I whispered. "Please…"

"Please, what?" He ran the tips of his fingers

around the top of my legs, over my ass, everywhere but where I needed him.

"Please touch me," I begged.

"Hmmm," he mused. He pulled his hand out of my panties and for a moment I thought he'd step away. Instead, he pulled at the top of my leggings, tugged them halfway down my legs. I kicked them the rest of the way off. My panties followed. "Tell me what you need," he whispered.

"I need your hand on my clit," I said, my mouth dry. Not surprising, I think all the moisture in my body was now between my legs.

"What's the magic word?" He ran his fingers over my thighs again.

"Please." If he didn't hurry, I was going to scream. Maybe that was what he wanted. He obviously liked it when I begged.

His tongue traced my lower lip. "I like being called sir in class, but I think out of class, it might be appropriate too, especially now."

I was going to come without his help at this rate. "Please, sir."

I gasped as he plunged his fingers into me. With urgency and not a bit of gentleness, he rammed them in and out of me. I bucked against his hand and bit my lip from screaming in ecstasy. This was *exactly* what I needed right now.

Just before I came, he pulled his hand away. "Not just yet." He grabbed up my discarded leggings and used them to tie my wrists to each other. I had never been tied up or dominated like this before. I was beyond turned on.

I watched him move down my body, bit by bit. Slowly he pushed up my tank top and claimed a nipple with his mouth. He sucked for a few moments, then bit down on my tender skin. I cried out and my eyes watered, but I was no less aroused. An intense look on his face, he did the same with my other nipple.

"Please, sir," I panted. "I need to come."

He raised an eyebrow at me, then scooted down lower. He parted my legs and dove in, face first, his tongue lapping at my folds and clit.

"Mmmm, gods," I breathed. "Yes." The pressure built again. He looked up at me, eyes on mine while he licked and sucked at my tender, swollen bud. I bucked against his mouth. Gods, it felt so damned good. I didn't care that he was my teacher, my coach, or that anyone might walk in on us. All I knew was the feel of his hot mouth.

I couldn't contain the cry when I finally came,

heat washing over me and carrying me away for long, slow, intense minute.

I wasn't even down when he pulled away and wiped his face. He crawled up to untie my hands and toss me my panties and leggings.

"Sir?" I frowned at him. "You don't want to…fuck me?"

He swallowed audibly. I could tell by the erection tenting his pants that he did.

"Of course I want to," he said, his voice strained. "I can't… I shouldn't have… you deserve better than an asshole like me."

Before I could even respond, he'd jumped up, grabbed his towel and stormed out of the training room.

"Was it something I said?" I muttered to myself. I watched the door in case he changed his mind, but it stayed shut while I quickly pulled on my clothes and wrapped my towel around my neck. My body throbbed where he'd touched me. Some of the lust was satisfied, but not all of it, not by a long way. I wanted to have his cock inside me, to feel…

I shook my head. Man or woman, no meant no and he'd been very clear in that. If anything like this happened again, well, we'd see. For all I knew, he'd avoid me now. I hoped that wasn't the case. Just thinking about the things he'd done to me made my pulse race. He'd given me a little taste, but I wanted more, much more.

I sat on a bench to pull on my socks and shoes and thought about the things he'd said. Lust wasn't a normal reaction to being told someone had killed someone else, even for me. The logical response was to be repulsed, but I had meant it when I said I believed him. He didn't seem the kind to take a life for no good reason. I knew normals sometimes put paranormals in a position where we had no choice but to fight back. I'd heard this from my mother all my life. To hear it from someone else and have it be so raw, was something else. I suspected whatever had happened, it hadn't happened long ago.

I teased my lower lip with my teeth. Did I really want to know what had happened? Part of me knew it was none of my business. The rest of me knew I'd look into it. If nothing else, I wanted to know if it had anything to do with the strange things I had seen. Although I had no reason to assume they were connected, I had a feeling they were.

I tied my laces into precise bows and rose. If he hadn't come back by now, I suppose he wasn't going to.

I sighed to myself. I was going to need another

"extra-long" shower, even after that orgasm. "Damn it," I said to myself. "And damn you, sir."

I turned off the light and closed the door behind me. This would definitely complicate things, but I didn't care. His tongue was amazing.

10

ARIANA GAVE me a worried look over her coffee cup. "Are you sure you're all right?" she asked. She had been watching me with that expression for a couple of days now. I'd given her short answers whenever she spoke to me. Not rude—at least I hoped not— but as brief as I could get away with. Mostly my thoughts were occupied with Nash and the way he'd fled the room in such a hurry.

Him and study. I wasn't going to let my education suffer for the sake of a guy.

I ran a hand over my hair and sighed. "I'm sorry, I just—" How did I even begin to explain what had happened? Should I try? While there weren't any laws against screwing teachers, the academy might not look favourably on Nash for what we'd done.

Sure, I was a consenting adult, but he was the one who could fail me if he wanted to. To say he'd held all the power wouldn't be an exaggeration. It was a turn on that made me wet to think about, but it wasn't wrong. The fact I'd surrendered to him so fully…

And there went my mind, imagining me tied to his bed while he licked me from my… I cleared my throat. I probably shouldn't be thinking of him like that. Still, he was hot and I didn't regret anything. Not yet anyway.

I glanced around the busy dining hall, then I told her, without going into too much detail, what had happened.

She gaped at me. "You and—wow!" To my relief, she seemed impressed. I hadn't been sure she wouldn't go straight to the school board and tell on us. "Dyson, Kane and now him. I don't know how you do it. Guys just…" She mimed swooning.

I smiled, but it turned in a grimace. "Complicate the hells out of my life?" I suggested.

"That too," she grinned. "Isn't that what they're for? Although," she sighed, "the only one who has shown any interest in me is Hamish."

Now it was my turn to gape. "Oh? When did that happen?" Had I really been so caught up in my own drama I hadn't noticed what was going on with her? She was—well, my best friend here at the academy. I missed Jess though, now more than ever. She would have known what to do. No, she would have told me to chase all of the guys and to be sure to sleep with them as often as possible. I might not chase, but I was *trying* to do the latter. Well, as much as I could without throwing myself at them.

"Yesterday," Ariana replied. "He almost fell over my foot, then he asked me out for dinner."

"And?" I prompted. "Are you going?"

I..." She looked down at the table. "I thought about it. He seems nice and all, but he's not really my type."

"Oh." I nodded. "What is your type?"

She glanced back up, but before she could respond, Kane appeared beside our table. He stopped and stood with his hands in front of him. He toyed with his fingers, an obvious sign of nerves.

"Hey, Peyton, I was wondering if... um. Sorry, am I interrupting something?" His face turned adorably pink.

"Yes," I said.

At the same time, Ariana said, "No."

"Uh..." He stood looking awkward and licked his

lips. "Maybe I should come back later." He took a step back.

"No, stay. It's fine, really," Ariana said. She swallowed the last of her coffee and rose. "I should get going anyway, I have an essay to write." She wrinkled her pretty nose. "The history of magic is interesting, but I wish I could use magic to write essays." She shook her head and hurried away.

"I'm sorry, I didn't mean to interrupt," Kane said. He settled into the chair beside mine.

I shrugged. "It's okay, I can catch up with her later. Did you want something?"

"Yes," he replied immediately. "I mean, I—" He swallowed, but I didn't miss the hungry look he gave me. "I wanted to ask you something."

My pulse raced. Maybe the pretend voice of Jess in my head was right, I should jump into things more. "Yes," I replied firmly.

"Yes?" he echoed. "But you don't know what I'm going to ask."

"Are you asking me out? If so, then yes. If it's something else then I've probably just made a fool of myself." I laughed awkwardly.

"Oh, I was." He tapped his fingers nervously on the tabletop. "I—really, you will?"

"Of course, I've been waiting for you to ask. If

you hadn't, I would have done it." Maybe. If I ever worked up the courage.

His blush deepened. He really was too stinkin' cute for his own good. "Great."

"Yeah. Um, so, did you have a date and time in mind?" I cocked my head at him.

"Oh, yes. Tonight. I have two tickets to a band. It's nothing big, just a pub band. I just thought…"

"That sounds perfect," I assured him. "I love live music."

"Me too." He grinned. "I'll pick you up from your room at eight."

"I'll put it in my phone." As if I would possibly forget.

I pulled it out of my pocket and turned on the screen. I brought up the calendar app and pressed on today's date.

The screen went black.

"Fuck, not again." I tapped at the screen. Where I touched, something appeared. I peered at it closer. "What the hells?"

"What is it?" Kane asked.

"I don't know. It looks like there's something in my phone." I lowered it so he could look. In place of the screen, or just blackness, vague shapes moved across the glass.

"What the… I've never seen anything like that before." He pressed a finger on the screen. The shapes surged toward his finger. He pulled it back and they dispersed. "That's fucking weird."

"You're telling me." I told him about the first time this had happened. "It wasn't quite like this though. I —" The screen went black and then flickered back to the normal, white screen of my calendar.

I placed the phone down on the table and watched it for a while, but nothing else abnormal seemed to happen.

"Is there any chance my phone is haunted?" I swallowed.

"I think that would only happen if ghosts were real," he replied.

"I wouldn't assume they aren't," I said uneasily. "I mean, we exist and apparently gargoyles and dragons too. The gods only knows what else might."

"That's true, I suppose." Dyson must have told him about the gargoyle. Or had I, while drinking one night? I couldn't remember. Either way, he knew. "Why haunt a phone though?"

"Why not haunt a phone?" I tapped the details of our date into the calendar and pressed "save." "They might be able to surf the net and watch porn."

Kane laughed softly. "I suppose they might."

I eyed him sideways. "Is that what you would do?" I asked teasingly.

"Um, I might." His throat bobbed. "Or stalk my brother on social media. If I die any time soon, it's probably going to be his fault somehow."

He gave me such a wry look, I burst out laughing.

"He is a lot to handle," I agreed. Not that it was a bad thing, in any way. Okay, maybe in a twin, but not in a guy friend-slash-whatever we were.

Kane sighed. "I know he doesn't mean to be. He's just…outgoing."

"Right." Without thinking, I leaned over and pressed my lips lightly to his. It was nothing like the heated kiss with Dyson or the unbridled lust with Nash. This kiss was sweet and soft. Kane tasted of some kind of spices I couldn't identify.

I sat back and licked my lips.

Kane looked stunned.

"I'm sorry, I shouldn't have assumed," I said softly. "I didn't think."

"No, it's all right," he said quickly. "I liked it."

"Really?" Thank the gods for that.

"Really." He raised a trembling hand to my cheek and ran a finger over it. Slowly, so slowly, he sat forward and kissed me, a little more firmly this time.

I decided it was cinnamon he tasted like. Maybe

some nutmeg thrown in there. He tasted better than a pie. I could have gobbled him down, then and there. Instead, I pulled back and smiled.

"That was nice," I told him.

He smiled. "It was nice for me too." He looked as though he had more to say, but he said nothing. He took my hand in his and kissed the centre of my palm. For such a sweet gesture, it sent a jolt of heat right to my core.

If I was Jess, I might drag him under the table and screw him then and there. I wasn't though, and phones had cameras. If there was anything I knew about this place it was that everyone had a phone, even the shifters.

I swallowed and forced pure thoughts into my dirty mind. One or two managed to stick. My mind objected to too much cleanliness. Life was too short for that.

"I should go and get ready for our date then," I said once my head was clear enough for me to risk speaking.

"Me too," he agreed. He looked like a man who had stumbled onto a pile of good luck and didn't know what to do with it. Gods, I hoped I didn't disappoint him.

He glanced down at my phone and frowned. "You

should probably take that to Madame Luc. Just in case there's something strange going on with it. It might just be a software glitch."

"It's possible," I agreed. "Or one of the social media platforms is using some new tech to stalk its users." If that was the case, all their users would be in an uproar. Then they'd go back to using it as though nothing had happened. People were, if nothing else, good at denying the existence of a problem until it impacted them directly. Even then…

"Yeah." He touched my screen with a fingertip, but it did nothing but turn on the screen and ask for my passcode. "It seems fine now."

I grinned.

"What?" he asked.

"I was just wondering if your brother would pretend to be sucked into the phone, just for shits and giggles."

Kane smiled wryly. "That's exactly something he would do," he agreed. "Maybe I should have. He keeps telling me to lighten up."

I cocked my head at him. "I like you just how you are." And I liked Dyson and even Nash. When did things get so messy?

"I like you how you are too," he replied. He rose

and offered me his hand. "Just think about what I said about Madame Luc."

"I will," I agreed. I had some time before our date. Maybe I would speak to her first, if only to put both of our minds at rest.

"Really? I mean, good." He nodded vigorously.

"Really," I assured him. I guessed Dyson brushed him off whenever he made any suggestions like that. Poor guy, it must suck being a twin at times. Or being a sibling of any kind. Twins didn't necessarily have the monopoly of being jerks to each other.

I tucked my phone into my pocket, but to be honest it made me feel uneasy. If it was haunted, then I had a ghost near my ass. If it wasn't, then I had something else weird near my ass. Call me crazy, but I kinda liked my butt. It was one of my better features. I preferred it un-haunted or possessed by phone demons or social media software.

"See you in a couple of hours." He gave me a quick kiss on the cheek and slipped away.

I smiled and headed in the opposite direction.

I KNOCKED on the open office door and peeked inside. "Madame Luc?"

"Oui?" She looked up from behind her desk and tucked some hair behind her ear. "Yes, come in. Uh, Peyton Chapel, am I correct?"

"Yes, Madame," I replied. "That's right." I stepped into the doorway. "I'm sorry to bother you, but I think I have a problem with my phone. I was hoping you could help."

Her office was tiny. I could probably have touched the opposite walls with my fingertips. All it contained was a small desk, a computer and a filing cabinet. No books; not one.

Welcome to the digital age.

"Yes, yes." She held out her hand. "What is the

problem?"

I handed her my phone and told her what I'd seen. "It's done it twice that I know of, but it's never done it before."

She raised the phone until it almost touched her nose. She tilted it this way and that, then lowered it and touched the screen. It turned on as normal. She held the phone toward me so I could enter the passcode, then looked through the settings. She frowned as she pressed and swiped and pressed again.

"Could it be a glitch?" I asked. "Or a virus?" I tucked my hands into my pockets. The idea someone might have done this on purpose made me want to grind my teeth.

"Possibly," she replied. She frowned at the phone in a way that didn't fill me with confidence. "Devices can behave in peculiar ways. Sometimes we find out why, sometimes we don't." She glanced up at me, then back as something loaded.

"Right. Maybe it won't happen again." I shrugged. "Or I should get a new one."

"Perhaps." She turned the phone off and handed it back. "I can see nothing wrong. No strange settings or apps. Your storage capacity looks normal for what you have on there. You might want to delete some photographs though. You may find it works faster with more memory available."

I grimaced. I was probably attached to all four thousand of the photos I had on there.

Maybe.

Okay, I could stand to get rid of three or four of them. Maybe five.

"What do I do if it happens again?" I asked.

"See if you can take a screenshot, or have a friend record it." She leaned back in her chair. It groaned in such a way I thought it might break and send her crashing into the wall behind her. Fortunately, it held. You'd think an academy which could give out phones could afford decent chairs. Priorities.

"In the meantime," she continued, "I wouldn't worry too much. It should be fine." She started to nod, but something in her expression made me wonder if she was being completely honest with me.

"All right, thank you." I backed up into the corridor just as she closed the door.

I caught the words, "You are welcome," before she closed it completely. I stared at the door for a moment before I turned away and almost ran into the guy who had stared at me at the party.

Close up, he was even better looking than he was at a distance, but his expression was stony.

"Um, sorry," I muttered.

"Look where you're going, and you don't have to be." His voice was as cold as the look in his eyes. Like he was at the party, he was dressed from head to toe in black. Everything fit him perfectly, which was to say a little too tight, so his biceps bulged out of his short sleeves. I'd bet his jeans hugged his ass, but I couldn't very well check from here.

I opened my mouth to offer some sort of explanation, but his tone rubbed me the wrong way.

Instead, I retorted, "You should take your own advice. You could hurt someone if you run into them."

He curled his lip at me. "*Please*, I'm not that clumsy." The accusation that I was, hung in the air between us like the invisible but toxic fog that comes after taco Tuesday.

I swear, if he could have shot lasers out of his eyes, he would have. I'd be incinerated on the spot. Nothing left but a pile of ashes. Smoking hot ashes, but still… Unfortunately for him, I could have used magic to knock him on his ass. Fortunately for him, I didn't want to get in trouble for doing it.

"Whatever," I snapped. "Are you going to move out of the way? You're taking up half the corridor." Yeah, that was an exaggeration, but I didn't care. He pissed me off and I wanted to be away from him, but in a way that didn't look like I was intimidated.

He laughed, but it was a bitter sound, not one of humour. "You could move out of *my* way."

"For fuck's sake," I growled. "What are you, a four year-old?"

"I was thinking the same thing about you," he replied coolly. "Are you old enough to be here?"

"No, I'm a fucking prodigy." I planted a hand on my hip and squared my shoulders back. "I'm really twelve."

He mimed my posture. "You certainly act like it."

I dropped my fist. "How the hells would you know how I act? You've just met me."

He shrugged with one shoulder. "I've seen you around."

"Yeah, at the party the other week. Why were you staring at me?" I narrowed my eyes at him.

He hesitated. "I was looking *past* you." He was a crap liar.

"Bullshit." I smirked. "You were looking straight at me."

He averted his eyes from mine. "I've never seen anyone with green hair before."

There was more, I could tell, but I wasn't going to get it from him. To be honest, I wasn't bothered to try. Who cared why he was looking at me? He was obviously an asshole. One I'd given enough time to already.

"Yeah, well, get used to it." So far, it hadn't grown out, even at the roots. I should have asked Madame Luc about it. I made a mental note to do that later. I really did prefer I not have a streak of emerald hair for the rest of my life.

"It doesn't sound like you have gotten used to it." Now he sounded amused, but totally at my expense.

Fucker.

"That's none of your business." I put a hand on my hair and shoved past him.

He laughed—*laughed*—at me. I watched him out of the corner of my eye, his face only a hand's width from mine, before I put him behind me.

I rounded on him. "Has anyone told you you're a jerk?"

He grinned, but there was nothing warm about it. "Frequently. It's kinda my thing."

"Obviously," I snapped.

He crossed his arms over his chest. He looked muscular under his black t-shirt, but only if I was looking. Which I wasn't. Much. Okay, a bit. But not too much, since he was an asshole. "Yeah. What's your excuse?" he asked.

I smiled sweetly. "I'm perfectly nice, unless you rub me the wrong way."

He leaned in closer to me. His breath caressed my cheek. He smiled of musk, and strangely, pizza. A tasty combination on anyone else. Okay, on him too, but I didn't want to dine at this table.

He spoke in a whisper. "I think you prefer to be rubbed the *right* way."

I pushed him back with my fingertips. "Of course I do, but I'm particular about who does the rubbing. Assholes need not apply." Although, where did that leave things with Nash? He claimed to be one himself. He certainly acted like it sometimes. He was different though, I decided, because I knew there was a good guy under there somewhere. This guy— he seemed like jerk, through and through. And through.

"You don't know what you're missing," he told me. "There's nothing more fun than an angry fuck."

"You've got the angry part down pat." My gaze scanned him up and down. "I'll pass on the fuck though. You don't seem like you know how to satisfy a lover." That was a flat-out lie. He looked like a guy who knew exactly what he was doing. I had to bite my tongue to keep from licking my lips.

He snorted. "Right back at you."

I smiled, flipped him off and said, "Fuck you."

"You wish."

"Not a chance." Why was I still standing there talking to this guy anyway? "What's your name?"

He appeared surprised by the question. "Matt. Why?"

"Because it's more satisfying to say your name when I tell you to get lost." I cleared my throat dramatically. "Fuck off, Matt. See, much better."

He rolled his eyes. "You wish, *Peyton*."

Now I was the surprised one. "How do you know my name?"

He looked smug. "I made a point of learning who to avoid."

My mouth dropped open. He really was a whole new level of dick. "And yet, you can't get out of my way in a corridor."

"That wasn't my fault," he said.

I started to retort but closed my mouth and shook my head. "I've wasted enough time on this conversation." More than enough. I should be in the shower right now.

"Funny, I was thinking the same thing," he remarked.

"That you've wasted my time?" I asked. "At least we agree on that."

He rolled his eyes and opened his mouth, but I turned away before he could speak.

With hurried steps, I headed away, toward my room. I muttered to myself as I went. It got me a few stares of confusion or amusement, but I ignored them. It was what I did when I was particularly annoyed. This—Matt—had me at a whole new level of irritated. I'd met all kinds of people in the past, and the gods knows we can't like everyone, but this was different. If I didn't know better, I would think he had gone out of his way to be objectionable. Like —he'd followed me and lurked around in the corridor so he could almost run into me and insult me.

Of course, this whole line of thinking was totally insane. Who would bother to do such a thing to another person? Oh yeah, stalkers. But aren't stalkers usually crazed admirers? Apart from suggesting we sleep together *because* we didn't like each other—and I'm pretty sure he was joking about that—he obviously didn't like me at all. We all have those people we take an instant dislike to, right? I know I have met a few. That could be all this was. Something still niggled at the back of my mind though, something I couldn't put a finger on.

I chewed my lip and pulled out my phone to

unlock my door. I thought back to the gargoyle and the warning I assumed they'd been trying to give me. Could they be warning against Matt? If they had, I got the message loud and clear. Stay away from the guy. If that was what the gargoyle had tried to tell me, they could have sent a text.

"Stay away from hot, but toxic guys who only wear black," I muttered. That was pretty good advice, right there. I made a note to follow it from now on. That didn't stop me from thinking about him when I got into the shower and wondering what his body looked like under his clothes.

I rinsed the idea away with my shampoo and followed it down the drain with my eyes. I would focus instead, on my date with Kane. That, I was looking forward to.

I smiled and got a mouthful of shampoo. While I spat and rinsed, I made another note—keep your mouth shut in the shower.

Also good advice. See, I could be wise, once in a while.

1 2

I WAS STILL FUMING when Kane knocked on the door. Ariana must have ducked in and out while I was in the shower. Some of her stuff had been moved around, but only a hint of the perfume she preferred remained.

I took a deep breath before I turned the knob and opened the door. Naturally, that set off a coughing fit. My mouth still tasted of shampoo. I must have swallowed some of it. At least my insides would be squeaky clean.

Kane stepped inside and patted my back while I doubled over, my hand over my mouth.

"Are you all right?" He grabbed my water bottle from the table beside my bed and handed it to me.

I took a gulp, then another, and managed to nod.

"Yes, I'm fine, thank you. I just like to choke on air from time to time."

He chuckled but looked as though he wasn't sure if he was supposed to do that or not.

I gave him a watery smile and placed my bottle back on the table. At least now I had forgotten about Matt. Oops, now he was in my head again. I shoved the thought of him away and smiled brightly.

"You look very handsome." He really did. The faded jeans with holes in the knees and fitted, blue t-shirt made me almost drool on the floor. I say "almost" because I turned away to grab my bag and wiped the side of my mouth so he couldn't see. Classy, that was me.

When I turned back. His face was pink, but he smiled broadly. "You're looking amazing yourself."

"Thanks," I mumbled. My skirt hung to just above my knees and my t-shirt was low cut to show a hint of cleavage. Not too much, I didn't want to look desperate. Be quiet, I wasn't *that* bad. Yet.

I'd put my hair up in a ponytail, taken it out and put it back up at least a dozen times since I dried it. It was currently down, so I guessed that's how I'd be wearing it tonight. Just in case, I grabbed a hair tie and slid it down my wrist.

"Okay, I'm ready," I said.

"Great." He gave me a look like he'd prefer to peel off all my clothes slowly and lick honey off my... He cleared his throat. "I guess we should go then."

"Yes, we should."

We stood and gazed at each other for a while longer. Finally, I stepped toward the door and opened it. "After you."

His eyes widened. "I'm sorry, I think that should have been my line."

I smiled and shrugged with one shoulder. "I'm an independent girl, I can open a door." I waved him out ahead of me and closed it behind us.

"All right, but let me get the next one," he said.

"If you insist."

He did insist, apparently. He opened every door between us and the pub, or he would have, but there was only the front one leading out of the academy and the one which led into the pub. The latter was already open.

We flashed our licences to the bored bouncer who only glanced at Kane's. He didn't even look at mine. I wasn't sure if I should be insulted or not.

"Would you like a drink?" Kane shouted over the throbbing music.

"Sure!" I shouted back. I grabbed his hand and led

him toward the bar to order our drinks. Beer for him, bourbon and cola for me.

He yelled something I couldn't hear. I gave him a confused look and shrugged. He tried again. Once again, I shook my head.

"I can't hear you!" I yelled.

"What?" He looked exasperated, took my hand and led me to a door at the back of the pub, which opened onto the beer garden. "I said the band is out here."

"Oh. Gotcha." At the side of the garden—really just an outdoor space with tables—a wooden platform was covered in speakers, drums and various other band-related stuff. A couple of guys and a girl were occupied settings things up and testing instruments and sound.

"Let's sit."

I followed Kane to a table at the back of the garden, furthest from the band.

"I'm pretty sure we'll hear them from here." He slid onto a bench and moved over to make room for me.

"I'm pretty sure we'd hear them at the academy," I said with a grin.

He chuckled. "Probably."

I nestled in a little too close and he casually slung an arm over my shoulders.

"This is, um, nice," I said. His fingers were a hair from my breast.

"It is. I'm glad I got some time alone with you. Well, sort of." He waved a hand at the crowds which had started to flood in and fill the tables. Before long, it was standing room only and the band started up.

They played a few classic pub anthems and we sang along and grooved to the music. Every so often, Kane's hand would touch my nipple and send a jolt of heat though me. After a while, I forgot to listen to the band and was focusing on him instead. I suspected he was completely oblivious until he did it again and blushed. This wasn't just a casual brush past this time though. He rubbed the tips of his fingers over my sensitive peak.

Dear gods. I bit back a moan and wriggled so my ass was pressed against his groin. His erection grew until it was poking into me.

It was dark in this part of the garden and everyone but us was focused on the band. No one saw him slip his hand inside my shirt and under my bra. He caught my nipple between his thumb and forefinger and rolled it gently.

I let out a ragged breath and wriggled against him again. He pulled his hand out of my shirt and moved it down under the table.

No way, he wasn't going to…

He touched my thigh, then moved his hand over between my legs.

I swallowed and looked around to make sure no one was paying any attention to us. They weren't. I parted my legs and let his fingers dive down between them.

He rubbed against the front of my skirt, lightly at first, then more insistently.

"If you keep that up, I'm going to—" I panted.

"I want you to," He said in my ear.

Oh. My. Gods.

I licked my lips but didn't object when he tugged my skirt up a little more. He slipped a hand underneath and rubbed against the front of my panties.

I was so aroused by now I barely cared if anyone was watching. Still, I glanced around to double check. Nope, all eyes were on the band, or the other people at their tables.

With a ragged breath of his own, Kane worked my panties aside and touched my heated core.

I bit back a moan. I wanted to buck against him

when he worked my clit, but I dare not do more than rock slightly.

"Come for me," he said in my ear.

And I thought he was the shy, quiet one. Well, you know what they say about them—they're usually the most outrageous.

I bit my lip. My head swum and stars danced above my head. He worked me a little harder, a little faster.

"Mmmm," I moaned. "I... I..." I came against his hand. My breath came out my nose in soft little pants. Pleasure washed over me, making the blood pound in my ears louder than the music.

I finally came down from my high and sagged again him.

"Good girl." He pulled his hand back out and tugged my skirt back into place.

I fixed my shirt while I caught my breath. "Should we finish this somewhere private?"

"Unless you want to stay and watch the band play," he said. His erection still pressed into my back, but he didn't sound as though he was in a rush.

I swivelled around to face him. "You really got off on that, didn't you?"

He smiled awkwardly. "Making you feel good? Yes."

"I mean, with all of these people here." I jerked my head toward them.

He licked his lips. "If they wouldn't kick us out, I'd strip down naked and take you on the table top."

His words aroused me all over again. I wasn't sure I could be that daring, but the idea of all those people watching us…

Oh gods.

"Is it the people or the thrill that we might get caught?" I asked.

He considered for a moment. "Both. I'm usually the one who doesn't get noticed." He grimaced at that. Of course he wasn't, Dyson was the one who paraded around naked. Apparently it ran in the family, but Kane hadn't acted on it yet. That I knew of.

"That would get you noticed all right." I could just imagine the kind of porn he preferred; groups and public places. At least we could do the latter. "I think I saw an alley on the other side of the pub."

A smile lit his face. "You'd be game?"

"Let's find out." I rose and offered him my hand.

He took it and we hurried out the rear entrance, past another bored bouncer. This one gave me a look which suggested maybe he had seen Kane with his hands up my skirt. My face heated, but I gave him a smile as we walked by.

The alley was pitch dark but joined the back of the pub to the busy street. I could have made a bubble of magic around us to hide us, but I didn't want to. Anyone could walk through at any moment. That made it all the more exciting.

No sooner had we stepped into the shadows that Kane's hands went up my shirt to caress my breasts and tease my nipples. He pulled down one side and my bra cup with it and leaned in to run his tongue over my hard peak.

I undid his jeans and tugged them down just enough to free his erection. Just as I suspected, his cock was big, like Dyson's, and rock hard. I ran my hand up and down his warm length. He moaned and grabbed on to my waist.

"I don't want to come in your hands," he said breathlessly.

I didn't want that either, I wanted to have him inside me. Now.

He lifted the front of my skirt and tugged down my panties. They fell to my feet and I kicked them off.

He turned me so my back was to the wall and put a hand under my leg to bring it up to his waist. I guided the tip of his cock to my opening and moved my hand out of the way.

He groaned and pressed himself into me. We both let out a moan then and stood like that for a full minute. Then he began to move, thrusting in and out of me with a careful rhythm. With every thrust, he hit me inside and out and drove me toward another orgasm.

"You feel so good," he breathed.

"So do you."

With his spare hand, he kneaded my breast, massaging my nipple and driving me closer and closer to the edge.

With all the noise coming from inside the pub, no one could hear me, so I didn't hold back little moans and sighs as I reached the edge of the precipice. I lifted my chin and cried out as another wave washed over me, filling my body with pounding, heated sensation.

Kane followed me a moment later, thrusting harder and harder into me, before he gripped my breast and let out a series of grunts.

Finally, he relaxed his posture and leaned his forehead on mine as we caught our breath.

A cough made me jump and I looked up as a

couple of people walked past. I had no doubt they'd gotten a good look at my exposed breast.

Oops.

They walked on by without stopping, but they both looked back a few times. Part of me wished they'd seen more.

Kane pulled out of me, dropped my leg and pulled up his jeans. He gave me a long look, as though he wanted to drink me in. "I've never met anyone like you," he whispered. He kissed me lightly on the mouth. "I'll walk you home," he said softly

I tugged my shirt back into place. Maybe I should feel weird about this, but I didn't. Not even a little bit.

13

"Today, we are working on something more complicated." Madame Luc declared.

After a couple of months at the academy, we had
all mastered the art of moving things with our
phones. The guy with the shaved head—Mustafa—
learned how not to lift himself by accident. That was
fortunate since his nose would have ended up mush
eventually.

We had also learnt how to knock each other
back. Hamish's arm had healed after being broken
when he was thrown into a wall a bit too hard. As
witches and wizards, we learnt how to blast people
back to protect ourselves. Now we had to learn how
to hold back, to control the exact amount of magic

we used. Learning restraint, it turns out, is much harder than learning to use magic in the first place.

"On your phones, go to the usual website and click on lesson seven." The lecturer paced in front of the room. She seemed agitated today. Every lesson had become progressively more difficult, but we'd eventually managed them all, if not mastered them. What was so different about seven that looked like she walked on pins and needles.

I glanced at Ariana and we both shrugged and clicked on the lesson.

"Oh," I said softly.

"You will see," Madame Luc said, "that you have options. Due to the space in this room, we will work one at a time. Everyone push your tables to the back of the room."

We did as instructed and stood milling about. Everyone looked as nervous as I felt.

"You," Madame pointed at Mustafa. "You go first."

"Um." He rubbed at his nose. His hair had grown out a little and now stood in spikes on his head. "Okay." He stood apart from us, scrunched up his face and clicked on his phone.

A shape appeared in the open space to the side of the room. It writhed and danced like it was obscured by flames and smoke.

Mustafa's face creased in a deeper frown.

The shape coalesced a little more, into—of all things—a goat. The goat bleated but looked out of focus. It took a few steps forward and latched onto the jacket of one of the students, Violette Ying.

"Hey, it's real!" she squealed as the goat took a chunk out of the garment and started to chew it.

The class cracked up laughing, including Violette. That was until she inspected the damage more carefully. "Hey, that was a new jacket, you stupid fucking animal."

"Tut-tut, language, mademoiselle," Luc scolded. She couldn't punish her for swearing, since this was university, but that didn't mean she liked us doing it.

"Sorry Madame," Violette said, "but it was expensive."

The goat finished chewing and lunged at Violette for more just before it disappeared entirely.

"Why did you choose the goat?" Violette asked, glaring daggers at Mustafa.

"I dunno," he replied, "I thought it'd be fun."

She grunted and muttered something about, "Fucking goats, ruined a perfectly good…"

"Mademoiselle Ariana," Madame Luc waved in her direction. "You try. See if you can get yours to appear more strongly. And maybe no goats, eh?"

Ariana grinned. "I'll try." She tilted her phone so I couldn't see her screen, then clicked on it, a sly smile on her face.

"What did you—shit!" Mustafa ducked as he was swooped by a bird which appeared as if out of nowhere. "Bloody hell, Ariana." He threw himself under the nearest table and hid.

The magpie—a black and white bird famous for swooping during their breeding season—was more in focus than the goat but disappeared after only a minute and one swoop.

"I'm sorry!" Ariana exclaimed. "I thought it might perch and sing. I quite like the oodle-oodle sound they make."

"Yeah." Mustafa crawled out from under the table and seemed to be pulling together what dignity he had left. I felt sorry for him, but it had been funny. At least a little bit.

"Try to keep it for longer next time," Madame said. "Although the magpie may be efficient in distracting an attacker for long enough for you to run."

"Madame," I said, "my father has a tattoo on his arm. Wouldn't that be quicker than using a phone?"

"Oui," she replied, "but it's much more obvious. To use a device means you may not be detected as the one doing the magic. However, it is wise to have a—how do you say—backup plan."

I nodded. "I see, thank you."

"You are welcome. You may go next."

I wrinkled my nose. I should have seen that coming. Lucky I had already chosen my creature out of the long list of those I could try to conjure up. My finger hovered over it, while I drew magic from around me. A tiny bit came from the silver Celtic-style ring I wore on my right hand. Although it would replenish, I preferred not to suck it all out at once. I drew more from the wood in the tables. The magic from them was weak and sad from being so compressed when made and covered in gum ever since. The metal in the legs held more magic, so I took some from there too. What I really needed was a good tree, or a cow. Believe it or not, cows actually contain a lot of magic. Being animals and eating grass, they were the epitome of nature. Why do you think milk is so good for you, not to mention a good burger?

I concentrated my magic on my phone and pressed the screen.

There, in front of me, a dark shape formed. After a moment, it came into sharper focus.

"It's a gargoyle," Violette said in surprise. Or was it awe? Maybe both.

The gargoyle turned toward her and bared what looked like sharp, pointy teeth.

"Crap!" She dove under the table when it took a step toward her. It lunged and took a chunk out of the table above her head. She screamed. "Peyton, get rid of it!"

"I don't know how!" I replied. I frowned at it, willing it away, but it turned toward me instead.

"Oh shit." I backed away a few steps, but my back hit the wall. "Madame, what do I do?"

"You need to wait it out," she replied, much more calmly than I felt.

The gargoyle turned and started toward her, its gait a slow, deliberate lope.

"Can it kill people?" Mustafa asked from under the table. When had he gone back underneath? It didn't matter, it was probably a smart move.

"Oui," Madame replied. "It's created by magic, but it's very much real." She even looked calm. How did she manage that? "The question is, how long will it last, and how would you fight such a creature?"

That was two questions, but I don't think anyone cared just now.

"Run like hells?" Mustafa suggested.

The gargoyle turned toward him and slashed at the table with long claws. It left five deep gouges in the tabletop.

"Stop talking," Hamish suggested. "It keeps going after people when they—eek!" He dove under the table beside Violette.

We all fell silent. The gargoyle paused and looked around slowly. It seemed to take us all in, one by one. Perhaps it was trying to decide who the tastiest one of us was. Evidently, it decided on Ariana. It moved toward her.

She let out a squeak.

"I don't think not talking is working," I remarked.

The creature glanced toward me but continued to stalk Ariana. She sidestepped around the edge of the room, toward the tables. It followed slowly, toying with her.

Her face was white as a sheet now. Her eyes were huge.

I moved behind the gargoyle. It didn't look back, but I sensed it knew I was there. How the hells had I magically created an intelligent creature, I had no idea. That was a question for later, if we survived this.

Ariana backed into a corner and the gargoyle closed in. It licked it lips, or what passed for lips at least. The slurp it made turned my stomach. This motherfucker I had created wanted to eat my best friend for lunch. Or a snack. The gods knew how much gargoyles actually ate.

It raised a claw and reached toward her.

At that moment, something inside me snapped. Digital magic be damned, I needed the old-fashioned kind. I drew a little from each of my classmates and threw it at the gargoyle. The blast knocked it sideways, off its feet and into the wall. It grunted as it slammed into cold, hard brick.

There, that'll show you—shit.

The gargoyle rose to its feet and shook like a dog after a bath. If the dog was pissed off enough to take your head off, that was. Hey, some dogs really, really hate being bathed.

It bared its teeth and started toward me like it was on a mission. It didn't just want to eat me, it wanted to grind my bones into dust and lap up every last drop of my blood. Not necessarily in that order. I saw that in its eyes, and more.

"Hey." I gave it a wave. "What's up?"

The gargoyle paused and cocked its head in confusion.

"Nice weather we're having," I said. "Well, if you

like winter that is. It a bit cold out there, to be honest."

The gargoyle hissed.

"Yeah, a lot of people feel that way about winter," I agreed. "Personally, don't mind it."

The gargoyle growled.

I swallowed. I didn't know if it understood me, but I kept on talking, trying to distract it. "Aren't gargoyles supposed to be protectors? Why are you attacking us? Shouldn't you be defending us?" From what, I didn't know, maybe the goat or the magpie.

The gargoyle's growl deepened.

"That's what I thought."

It lunged and I threw myself to one side. I hit the floor hard and threw my arm up over my face. I screwed my eyes closed tight and waited.

Nothing happened.

I cracked open one eye, then the other. The gargoyle was gone.

"Well, that was different." I tried to stand, but my knees refused to hold my weight, so I stayed the floor and shook for a while.

"That was close." Mustafa looked as if he might spend the rest of the class under the table.

"Oui," Madame replied. "Magical creatures can be hard to control."

"You think?" Violette grunted.

"The situation was always well in hand." Madame's tone was curt. "This room is designed to protect against magic. None can get in or out."

"So, it could have killed us, but not left the room?" I asked.

"Precisely," Madame replied.

"Bloody hells, the liability insurance on this pace must be through the roof," I muttered.

"Oui," she agreed, "but how else are you to learn?"

"Maybe we should have started by creating something harmless?" Ariana said. "Like a turtle."

"Turtles bite," Mustafa said.

"Well… a kitten then," Ariana replied.

"Kittens also bite," Violette said. "And scratch."

"At least they don't try to eat your face," I pointed out.

"Oui, no more gargoyles in the classroom. I will have to contact the site and have them remove that option." Madame sniffed. "All right, who is next?"

1 4

"HEY, SEXY."

After the class with the gargoyle, I was much more cautious of the one I had seen on my date with Dyson. I was jumpy too. So much so that when Dyson appeared at my elbow and spoke suddenly, I jumped almost out of my skin.

I pressed a hand to my chest, over my racing heart. "Dear gods, don't sneak up on a person," I said, once I'd caught my breath.

He grinned. "Sorry."

I narrowed my eyes at him. "You don't look sorry."

His grin just widened as he draped his arm over my shoulder. "I heard you created a monster," he said casually.

"No, I just *met* you," I said sweetly.

He threw back his head and laughed. "I guess I deserved that after scaring you."

"Damn right you did," I told him. Then I sighed. "You're right though." I filled him in on the whole gargoyle thing while we walked through the academy.

He looked thoughtful. "A magically created creature and a shifter are very different animals, generally speaking. Assuming the gargoyle we saw was a shifter, then you'll only be in danger if he wants you harmed."

"And if it was created by magic?" I asked. "Blasting it didn't seem to do much of anything to the one I conjured. It shook it off like I'd shoved it with my hand."

"It wouldn't matter if it was a gargoyle or a unicorn. If it was created to attack you, it will." Dyson shrugged.

"That's reassuring," I said sarcastically. "Except I didn't create it to attack me." I frowned. "Not that I know of, anyway. I'm pretty sure I don't have a death wish."

"Most magical creatures just do what their nature tells them to," he said slowly. "A magical dog will bite, bark or pee on your leg. Same with a shifter, but only if you ask nicely." He grinned.

"Under no circumstances would I ask you to do that," I said dryly.

He pouted. "Shame." His eyes shone, so I knew he was joking. At least, I hoped he was. I didn't want to shame anyone for their kink, but this one wasn't one of mine.

He ran a hand over his hair. "Magically created creatures are usually only aggressive if that's their nature, or if the witch or wizard told them to. Then they'll attack whatever is in front of them."

"I don't recall telling the gargoyle to damage academy property," I said slowly. "Since gargoyles aren't real, as such, then the gods only know what their nature is."

"Aggression is usually part of the existing spell; the tattoo or in this case, the link. I'm not sure why an academic website would have it inbuilt like that. That seems—badly thought out."

I snorted. "Ya think?"

He laughed. "Just a little bit. Still, no harm done. Although, think nice thoughts next time you conjure up any creatures, just in case."

"You think I did it?" If I had imbued the gargoyle

with its not-so-charming personality without thinking, I wanted to know about it.

Dyson shrugged "It's possible. Magic isn't an exact science, especially when you're new to using it the way you're learning to here. Although, the gargoyle should have come with a failsafe embedded in the spell to make sure it didn't matter if you had. Or…"

"Or what?" I prompted.

"Or Madame Luc didn't expect any of you to be able to make the spell last for that long. One of my friends, when he took the class last year, could only make a butterfly appear for a matter of moments."

"Butterflies aren't known for living long," I pointed out.

Dyson looked surprised, then burst out laughing. "That's true," he said when he managed to contain himself. "But longer than his, I suspect."

"Did he ever learn to make them last for longer?" I might have to try to make mine last for less time, in case I conjured up something nasty again.

"Not really," Dyson replied. "Last I heard, he managed to make a snail, but someone else stepped on it before anyone could tell."

I wrinkled my nose. "That sounds messy."

"I suppose it would be. Dead magical creatures

tend to last longer than alive ones, for some reason, but they're virtually impossible to kill."

"I'll keep that in mind," I said. "If I create a gargoyle, I'll be sure to step on it."

Dyson chuckled. "No offence, but I don't think your feet are big enough."

"I would be offended if you said they were," I told him.

He looked down at my feet and shook his head. "They look perfectly normal to me."

"Thank the gods for that."

We reached my room and stood awkwardly the door for a few moments.

"Um, do you want to come in?" I asked. My heart raced. I liked him, a lot, and his brother too. Even Nash was in the back of my mind constantly. I had imagined how Dyson's hands would feel on me, his tongue, his… Would he be like his brother, or did he prefer to keep things more private? I suspected the latter. He had a more outgoing personality, but Kane was outgoing when it came to sex.

"Uh, thanks, but I should go. I have to, er, study." He held his hands loosely in front of him, like he was hiding a raging hard-on.

"Are you sure?" I asked. "I wouldn't mind some company."

"I'm sure," he said. "I don't like to rush things." For good measure, he leaned down to press a warm kiss against my lips. He deepened it after a moment. His tongue tickled along my lower lip.

When I opened my mouth to him, he pulled back. "Well, good night."

I dropped my eyes. Yep, that was an erection all right.

"Night. Sleep well."

"Yeah, sweet dreams." He shook his head and seemed to regain hold of himself again. "Don't forget to dream about me. And my dick." He winked and swaggered off down the corridor, leaving me confused and shaking my head.

I opened the door and closed it behind me. Ariana was sitting on her bed, headphones on her ears, grooving to music only she could hear. Just as well Dyson had declined. We would have had to find somewhere else to go anyway.

"Hey." I dropped my bag on my bed.

"What?" Ariana shouted. "Oh, sorry." She pulled off her headphones. "Did you say something?"

"No, just hello." I shrugged and flopped down beside my bag. I told her what Dyson had said about magical creatures.

Her eyes widened. "So in theory I could create an attack unicorn?"

I hesitated. Was that really what she took away from all of this? "I mean… I suppose so," I replied slowly. "Are you likely to want to do that?"

"Make an animal that can stab my enemies with its horn? That sounds pretty awesome to me," she enthused.

I cocked my head. "You have enemies?"

She gave me a lopsided smile. "Well, not exactly, but you never know what might happen in the future. Normals don't always like knowing paranormals exist."

"Right, but I don't want to kill them for it." I would defend myself if I had to. Maybe not with a unicorn. That gave me an idea though.

"We should get tattoos," I declared.

"I thought the idea of being here was…" She held up her phone.

"It is, but in a pinch we still need traditional magic," I said firmly. "You could have a unicorn tattooed onto your arm. Imagine how cute that would be."

She grinned and nodded vigorously. "With a pink mane? Oh no, rainbow!"

I pictured a rainbow unicorn on a killing spree

on her behalf and held back a laugh. It was a strange mental image, for sure.

"What would you have?" she asked.

I thought for a moment. As long as the spell was pointed in the right direction, then I should be all right… "Maybe a gargoyle," I said with a shrug. "They are kind of cool, when they're not destroying tables and trying to attack my friends."

Ariana made a face. "Maybe you should get something more benign, like a velociraptor or a bear."

Benign? I raised an eyebrow, but I understood she was being ironic. "Maybe a drop bear," I joked.

The idea that koalas turn into ferocious, carnivorous beasts was pretty funny. From what I gather, some international tourists still thought the myth was true. It's not. Trust me when I tell you, not all animals in Australia are trying to kill you. Unless, of course, a witch or wizard creates a magical attack koala.

I considered that for a moment but shook my head. Best not to perpetuate that rumour, tempting though it was.

Ariana giggled. "A kangaroo would be a formidable protector, with those powerful legs."

"True," I agreed, "but I really like the idea of having a gargoyle."

She nodded. "Okay, all we need is a tattoo artist who can do magic."

I rubbed my earlobe between my thumb and forefinger. "That shouldn't be too hard. Someone here will know where to find one. I'll shoot a message off to Kane."

"Or Dyson," she said. "I would think he'd be more likely to know."

"Yeah," I said slowly. "But things with him are weird."

"Oh." She leaned back against her pillows. "Maybe he's not into you like that."

I sighed. "I guess not, but I thought he was." Why did men have to be so damned mysterious?

I grabbed up my phone and sent a message to Kane. He replied a few moments later with an address nearby and a promise to take us there. That was followed by a photo of a tattoo in the shape of a snake. It was beautifully done, very intricate. It looked as though it might come alive at any moment. It couldn't, since he was a shifter and not a wizard, but it was still stunning.

I turned the phone to show Ariana.

"Unsolicited picture of his snake, hmmm?" she asked jokingly. Her eyes shone with amusement.

I snorted a laugh. "Better that than a dick pic." I liked the *feel* of his cock, but I didn't need a photo of it. Luckily, I suspected Kane wasn't the kind of guy who would send pics like that anyway.

I responded to Kane and put my phone on the table beside my bed. "Looks like we're getting inked."

I wondered if there was a magical hairdresser who could get rid of the green in my hair. I didn't say that out loud though. I knew Ariana had just been trying to help. At least she hadn't made me bald for life. Compared to that, what was a little bit of green?

I sighed again and got up to shower and change into my pyjamas. My dreams would be interesting tonight: gargoyles, drop bears, snakes and Dyson's dick. My subconscious was going to have a field day.

"A least you have someone to send you dick pics." Ariana sighed.

"Be careful what you wish for," I said with a grimace. "There's a whole internet out there full of guys ready to share their cocks with you." And the gods knew what else.

She stuck out her tongue in disgust. "Good point.

Never mind then. I think I'll stick to..." She shook her head and didn't finish her sentence.

I gave her a long look, in case she had more to say. She just pulled her headphones back over her ears and went back to grooving silently.

After a while, I stepped into the bathroom and closed the door behind me. There was definitely something going on with her, but I had no idea what. At some point, I hoped she'd open up to me and share. Until then, I would be here for her as much as she would let me.

I slipped under the water and let it rinse the frustration of her, and Dyson down the drain.

15

Uh, really?

"I'm supposed to trust you to put ink on my skin?" I stared at the tattoo gun in Matt's hand and grimaced.

"Not at all," he replied coldly. "You're free to go somewhere else if you prefer."

"You two know each other?" Kane looked from one to the other of us.

"Yeah, she almost ran into me because she doesn't look where she's going," Matt said, his eyes still on me.

I gave him a "fuck all the way off," look and said, "I was distracted. He didn't have to be a dick about it."

"She's a real charmer, this one." Matt smirked.

"Um, I could go first," Ariana offered. She held her phone in her hand and shifted from foot to foot. I knew she'd found a picture of the unicorn she wanted and was eager to have it on her skin.

I stepped back. "Be my guest." I waved my arm toward the chair.

She grinned and sat before showing Matt the screenshot she'd taken. If he thought it funny or strange, he gave no sign. Instead, he nodded and got to work.

In the meantime, Kane took my hand and led me over to the other side of the tattoo parlour.

"Are you all right? You seem upset. I know Matt can be a bit abrasive—"

"He's an asshole," I said quietly. "How do I know he won't ink a wombat on me instead?"

Kane tried to bite back a grin but failed. "That would be cute," he said, "but we're all here to watch and make sure you get what you want. Matt is a professional. He wouldn't risk his reputation just to be a dick to you."

I gave Kane a side-eye. "Are you sure about that?"

He looked uncomfortable. "If you hate him that much, we can go somewhere else. I know another place, but they aren't quite as good..." He jerked a thumb toward the door.

"I don't hate him," I said quickly. "I just think he's an ass. But if you trust him—"

"I really do." Kane pushed his sleeve up to reveal the snake he'd shown me the night before. In person, it looked even more impressive. "I only wish I could make it come to life too. It would be epic." He pulled his sleeve back down.

"Hey," I said, keeping my voice low. "You can shift. That's pretty amazing, you know. I can't do that."

I licked my lips and hoped he'd tell me what he could shift into.

He kneaded his hands. "I know, I should be glad for what I have."

"Something like that," I agreed. "How does it go— we always want what we can't have."

"Hey." He stepped closer to me. "Sometimes we want things we *can* have." He leaned in to nibble at my ear.

I writhed a little but didn't push him away. "That's true," I agreed. "But not here, in front of these two."

Kane blushed. "No, of course not, I wasn't thinking…"

He was thinking exactly that, I saw it in his eyes and the way the front of his pants stood to attention.

I smiled knowingly. My blood heated. "We might have to try to find a place."

He swallowed audibly. "Really?"

"Yeah, really." I had no idea where though. I couldn't just google, "public places suitable to have sex in," could I? Is that even a thing?

Go ahead and look, I'll wait.

It said something about parks or forests, didn't it? I filed that away for future thought.

"I like you," I told him. "A lot."

"I like you too," he replied. "You like Dyson too, don't you?"

"I do, but I don't think he feels the same way."

Kane looked perplexed. "I would say—"

He was interrupted by Ariana's squeal. We both jumped.

"Are you all right over there?" I called out and shot daggers at Matt with my eyes.

He ignored me, but she grinned.

"More than all right, it's amazing so far. Come and look." She waved us over as best she could without moving her opposite arm.

Honestly, the last place I wanted to be was closer to Matt, but I moved until I could make out the outline of the unicorn and its face. I had to admit, the detail was extraordinary.

"Did you make that with magic?" I asked.

"A bit of magic has gone into it, yes." Matt's tone was curt. "To make sure she does what she's supposed to. We don't want her to leap off and destroy half a classroom." He looked up and shot me a meaningful look.

Oh good, he knew about that. *Wonderful.*

I grimaced. "Make sure you do it right."

He looked up again, oh so slowly this time. "I always *do it right*," he said coolly.

The inflection was not lost on me. In fact, my stupid body responded to him in a more unwelcome way. Thank goodness lady boners weren't as obvious as dude boners.

"Mmm, I'm sure," I said, my mouth suddenly dry.

He looked away. "Are you going to let me do it to you next?"

"No way—" I started to say. I caught myself. "Oh, you mean the tattoo."

He snorted. "What else would I mean?"

"Nothing," I muttered. His expression was bland, but I sensed he was laughing on the inside. Would the world judge me badly if I took that tattoo gun and shoved it where the sun don't shine?

"It's very nice, Ariana," I told her.

She gave me a funny look but smiled. "This was a good idea of yours."

I wasn't so sure about that, but I returned her smile and watched as Matt added more detail. A hoof here, rainbow mane there. Before long, the unicorn looked as if it might really leap off her skin and wander around the tattoo parlour.

"You're very talented," I said without thinking.

"No shit," Matt replied without so much as glancing my way. "That's why you're here."

"Are you always so arrogant?" I asked, before Kane took my arm and pulled me back, away from him.

"It might be a good idea to let him concentrate," Kane said. "Otherwise he might make a mistake."

"Never going to happen," Matt said over his shoulder.

I curled my lip in his direction but turned away. "I'm sorry, he just—" I wasn't going to say, "rubs me the wrong way" again. I'd learnt my lesson after the first time. "He annoys me," I said finally.

"So I see." Kane turned me toward the front window and started to massage my shoulders. "He certainly is very sure of himself."

I dropped my chin to my chest and groaned. Gods, that felt good.

"That's one way to put it," I agreed.

"You're so tense," Kane said. He expertly kneaded out a knot or two and pulled my hair aside to kiss the back of my neck. "You don't have to do this, you know."

"I know." The feel of his lips sent heat through my entire body. "I want to."

"That's good, because it's your turn," Matt said.

Ariana smiled and showed off the unicorn which seemed to prance over her skin.

"It's very nice," I said. "I look forward to seeing it come alive some day."

"Are you fucking serious?" Matt snapped. "The only way that unicorn comes to life is if she's in danger. You would wish that on your friend?" He gave me a "what-the-hells-kind-of-friend-are-you?" look and turned away in disgust.

I gaped at him. "I just meant—"

"I don't care what you meant," he said, his tone curt. "Are you getting one done or not?" His eyes held a challenge. He was sure I'd walk away. He'd probably put money on it.

Fuck that.

"Since apparently you're the best, then I might as well." I flopped down in the chair while he gaped at me.

He sucked in a breath and let it out in a hiss. "Fine, what do you want and where do you want me to put it?"

There he went again with the innuendos.

Stick it where it fits, I thought sourly.

I smiled sweetly. "Same place as Ariana and this please." I held up my phone to show him.

His honey skin paled. "I…you…" He swallowed. "You want a gargoyle?"

"No, I want a fluffy bunny with a sweet little cotton tail," I said sarcastically. "Yes, I want a gargoyle. Is there a problem with that?"

"I…y…no. No." He squared his shoulders. "It's fine."

I exchanged confused glances with Kane. If there was some reason gargoyles bothered Matt, he clearly didn't know why either.

Ariana shrugged. "I said the same thing. I mean, the gargoyle she created could have killed us all. That's our Peyton for you, always keeping life interesting."

Our Peyton?

"Yeah well, I'd like to have a gargoyle I can control," I said lightly.

Matt twitched. "As if you'd control a gargoyle," he said derisively.

"Oh? I didn't realise you were an expert." I said.

"I'm not," he replied. "I just heard what happened in Madame Luc's class, that's all."

That was not all, but I wouldn't ask. For one thing, I doubted he'd tell me. For another, I didn't really care. He was probably just behaving this way to piss me off.

I leaned back and pulled up the sleeve on my left arm so he could work.

"You want it just like that picture?" he asked. "Lots of black. Red eyes."

"Horns, wings, big ears," I said. "All of those things." Just like the one I had created and the one Dyson and I had seen on our date.

"Fine."

The tattoo gun stung as it touched my skin, but I forced myself not to flinch. The lower arm might not be the best place for a tattoo, in terms of pain, but I wanted it accessible in case I needed it. For that, a few minutes was worth it.

I gritted my teeth and watched carefully as he worked. Call me a cynic, but I didn't trust that he wouldn't ink a fluffy bunny onto my skin instead. Granted, an attack bunny might be pretty awesome, but I would look a lot less badass.

Bit by bit, a gargoyle started to appear on my

skin. First the outline, then the bits in between; eyes, mouth, claws, the insides of his ears. Or was that her ears? Either way, it looked even more impressive than Ariana's or Kane's tattoos.

Every so often, I glanced toward Matt. His eyes were focused on his work, mouth set in a hard line. A bead of sweat formed on his forehead. He must be trying very hard. Was it professional pride, some kind of interest in gargoyles, or because he didn't want to give me an excuse to bitch later? You know I would take it if he gave me one. Oh yes, I would.

"That's amazing," Ariana said breathlessly. She stood on my other side, her eyes wide and intent on my arm.

"It's okay," I said casually.

Matt flinched slightly and a frown crossed his brow. "It's more than all right," he growled.

"I guess it is," I said after a moment. "I'll tell you when you're done."

For a moment I thought he might actually stomp off and refuse to finish. He frowned more deeply and went on working until he sat back and set his tattoo gun down beside him.

"There." His gaze met mine and again they held a challenge.

I leaned down to inspect my tattoo carefully.

Eventually, I sat back and nodded. "I like it. Thank you."

After a few seconds, his frown lifted and was replaced with a smug look. "You're welcome. You know where to find me when you want a *bigger* one."

Again with the innuendos.

I smirked. "I'm perfectly satisfied with the one I have." With that I hopped up from the chair and let him interpret that however he liked.

16

"WHAT IS THAT?"

Nash hadn't spoken to me other than to instruct me since our—whatever that was. The fact he did now took me by surprise.

"It's a tattoo," I said coolly. Or at least, cool on the outside. Inside, I was a tumult of burning emotion and lust. In spite of him being aloof for weeks, my knees still turned to mush when he was close.

He snorted. "Obviously. What is it for?"

"What do you think it's for?" I replied, a bit more blunt than I had intended.

"So you can defend yourself," he stated. "Do you have that little faith in your skills?"

For some reason, his words stung.

"I have plenty of faith in myself," I retorted. "It's other people, other paranormals I don't have faith in."

"And?" he prompted.

I hesitated. "And how long it takes to pull out a device and use it."

He nodded. "It's never wise to rely on only one method of self-defence."

I cocked my head at him. "Why the third degree about it then?"

"Is that what you thought that was?" He looked at me through half-lidded eyes.

"What would you call it?" I grabbed up my towel and pulled it around my neck.

"I don't know." He picked up his own towel and started to walk away.

"I don't get you," I said to his back.

He stopped, but didn't look back. "What's to get?"

"Hells if I know," I said in exasperation.

He turned around slowly, his expression guarded. "Maybe there's a reason for that."

"Maybe there is." I stepped closer, moving slowly like I approached a wild animal. "You don't have to tell me, but I'm a good listener." I licked my lips. "I didn't tell anyone about the things you told me the last time."

"Peyton," he said softly. So softly my pulse raced faster. Gods, he was so close now his breath brushed my cheek. "I want you. That's the problem."

"I don't see why that's a problem," I said, my voice higher than usual. "We're both adults."

He swallowed. "I'm your teacher."

"Do you give me preferential treatment?"

"Gods," he said breathlessly, "I want to."

I could have melted on the spot. "Why don't you then?" We were almost eye to eye, nose and to nose. His breath brushed over my lips. I thought for a while he'd kiss me. I half closed my eyes.

"I can't." He stepped back away from me. "It's not just that I'm your teacher. I'm damaged, Peyton. Damaged in ways you couldn't begin to imagine or understand."

I wasn't going to let him walk away that easily. "Why don't you try me?" I pressed my fists to my hips and gave him a challenging look. "You said you took a life. Why?"

"It's complicated." He seemed conflicted, like he wanted to tell me, but was scared of what I'd think of him if he did.

"I have time." I had an assignment to write for my history class, but it could wait.

He opened his mouth, closed it again and shook

his head. "It's nothing a student needs to know about." Just like that, he closed up again, tight.

I hesitated, then let out a breath through pursed lips. "All right, but if you change your mind, I'm here for you."

"Yeah." He gripped the ends of his towel in tight, white fists and headed out of the training room.

I watched his perfect ass until he passed through the doorway. I headed for the showers. In spite of having a bathroom upstairs, attached to mine and Ariana's room, I preferred to shower down here after training. It saved me walking through the academy covered in sweat and meant Ariana didn't have to wait until I was done, to take her turn. Or vice versa.

I dragged off my sweats, dropped them on the floor and stepped under the warm flow. Like always, it washed the worst of my cares away, at least for now. Still, in the back of my mind was the lingering wonder about Nash and whatever darkness lurked around his soul. What was it with all these guys and their enigmatic personalities? First there was Dyson and his mixed signals, then there was Matt, who may or may not just be an asshole and last was Nash. Him I got the least of all. Matt, I didn't want to get, to be honest. The others though... They both intrigued me.

Not, I should add, that Kane didn't, but he seemed a lot more straightforward than the rest. Thinking about him and what he wanted to do with me made my mouth dry.

I turned off the water and stepped out to grab a towel. I wrapped it around myself and searched my bag for a pair of clean panties. Before I even found them, I heard footsteps outside the bathroom door.

Had I locked it?

The nob turned.

I started to search for my phone but gave up after a moment. I turned to face the door and held up my arm, ready to call the gargoyle if I needed it.

The door swung inwards. My breath caught in my throat.

"Nash?"

He stopped dead. "I was hoping you'd still be here."

"You changed your mind about talking?" I asked.

"No." He shook his head slowly and licked his lips. He shut the door behind himself and locked it.

Excitement burned through me like wild fire.

He closed the distance between us. He grabbed

my shoulders, turned me and all but threw me against the sink. I slammed my palms onto the counter.

He whipped off my towel and threw it to one side.

In the mirror, I watched him undo his jeans and push them down far enough to free his erection. A moment later, he had me bent over the sink and rammed himself into me, hard.

I gasped out loud.

"I told you I want you," he said with a grunt. "You drive me crazy."

I looked toward the mirror. My breasts swung with each thrust. His eyes were closed and his expression was one of pure bliss.

I closed my own eyes and enjoyed the feeling of him pounding into me, touching me deep inside. He reached around to find my clit and rubbed firmly with each thrust. I had already been extremely aroused, so his touch pushed me toward the edge like a raging rapid.

Before I could come, he pulled out of me, turned me around and lifted me onto the sink. He leaned in to lick one of my nipples, then sucked for a few moments before he drew my legs around his hips and slid back into me.

"You feel better than I could have imagined," he said, his voice rough. "And I did imagine this. And so much more."

"Oh?" From this angle, every thrust hit me inside and out. Only a handful more and I would topple over the precipice.

"Mmm," he replied. "Mostly I pictured you tied to my bed and letting me do whatever I want to you."

I moaned with the increased sensation his words sent all the way through me. "You like having power?"

"Oh yeah," he grunted. "I want you to give yourself to me, fully."

I wasn't sure what more I could do for him at this point. "What do you want?" I asked him. "What do you need? Sir."

He moaned. "Don't stop calling me that. When I fuck you, I want you to call me sir." He thrust harder, deeper.

"Yes, sir," I whispered. I was so close to cresting now.

"I want you to do what I tell you," he added.

"Yes, sir," I said again. I reached my peak and fell over the top into a pool of intense and powerful desire.

He pulled out of me and pulled me down from the sink. "Get on your knees," he ordered.

"Yes, sir." My head was still swimming, but I knelt in front of him.

He grabbed a handful of my damp hair and guided my mouth to his cock. "Take me in as deep as you can."

I couldn't respond now, with a mouth full of cock, but I managed a small nod.

"Deeper." He thrust into my mouth, almost to the back of my throat.

I tasted myself on him, but I sucked and ran my tongue over his length and tip.

He grunted and slid himself in and out, past my lips. "Your mouth is incredible," he breathed. He pounded a little faster, hips bucking, breath more and more ragged.

"Gods, Peyton…" He groaned loudly and came, squirting hot cum into my mouth and down my throat.

I swallowed a couple of times and kept sucking until I had milked him dry. Only then did he pull out of me and offered me his hand to get up.

"We probably shouldn't have done that," he said with a hint of regret, "but I don't want to stop. I know I'm not the only guy… you should see guys your own age…"

"I want to do that again too," I said, guessing where he was going with this. "I…" I blushed slightly. "I like when you get all bossy with me." For an independent girl, I actually enjoyed it when he dominated me. I wouldn't want Kane or Dyson to do it, but there was something about Nash that made me want to surrender myself to him, to let him touch me any way he liked.

He looked surprised but smiled. "Great. I'll get bossy more often then." He cupped my breasts and rubbed his palms against my nipples. "When we're apart, you do whatever you like, but when we're together like this, you're all mine." As if to empathise his words, he leaned in to claim my mouth. His tongue pushed past my lips and invaded my mouth with as much force as he'd used with his cock.

He moaned against my mouth, then stepped back. "I could be with you a million times and never tire of you." He pinched my nipples between his thumb and forefinger, until I flinched from the delicious pain.

"Of course, I'm that awesome," I joked.

He smiled. "Yes, you are." A shadow passed across

his face and he dropped his hands and stepped back. "Undeniably. And gorgeous."

"I don't know about that, sir," I said with a smile. I resumed my search for clean panties and pulled them on while he watched.

"I do," he said simply. He looked as though he couldn't quite believe what we'd just done.

I wasn't sure I did either. I had screwed a teacher in a bathroom at the academy. That was definately not something I had expected to do when I came here. Did I regret it? Hell no. He was hot and I would do it again. It wasn't as though we were getting married or anything.

I pulled on my bra and he hooked it up for me.

"A guy who knows how bras work," I said, "I'm impressed."

He chuckled. "I usually prefer to take them off, but I'll make an exception in this case. For now."

I smiled and tugged on track pants and a t-shirt. In spite of him being "bossy" this felt comfortable. Not like a teacher and a student, but like a man and a woman, with a genuine connection. Could it become something more? Only time would tell.

"Stay after training tomorrow," he said. "I want to give you extra training so you never need to use that gargoyle of yours."

"Do you have a tattoo?" I asked. I had yet to see one on him, although I had been looking.

"I don't need one," he said. Without explaining, he unlocked the door and stepped out of the room.

"IT REALLY IS STARTING to get complicated." I ran the tip of my finger around my tattoo and glanced up at Ariana. She lay stretched out on her bed, on her stomach, her headphones around her neck.

"Maybe you should just decide who you like the best and concentrate on them?" she suggested. She popped something into her mouth before holding the packet out to me.

I peered at the label. "Weed gummies?"

She shrugged. "They help me to relax and ease the pain from typing so much. Try one."

I put a hand up. "No thanks. Another time, maybe."

"All the more for me," she said breezily, but she

closed the packet and put it away in the drawer beside her bed.

I sat back against my pillows. "I don't know who I like the best," I admitted. "Kane is adorable. I could see myself falling for him. Dyson is… I don't know what he is, but I want to find out. Nash—" I licked my lips. "He's exciting."

Ariana didn't seem even slightly bothered by the fact he was a teacher. In fact, she had grinned when I'd mentioned him. Evidently, she had a rebellious streak I hadn't known about.

"I'm not saying you have to choose, but if you don't, then your life is only going to get more complicated," she said. "Sooner or later you'll have to pick one of them. If they care about you, the guys you don't choose will get hurt."

I sighed. "I know. I don't want to string anyone along, I just… I mean, we're just messing around right now. Nash said he doesn't care if I'm seeing anyone else."

"How does Kane feel?" she asked.

"He knows I like Dyson too. I haven't said anything to him about Nash." I winced at the idea.

"Then you should do that first," Ariana said firmly. "You don't want him to find out when he walks in on you."

I suspected Kane might enjoy standing back and watching, but I didn't tell her that. I nodded. "You're right, I should. I'm just not sure how I even start that conversation."

"Just be honest." She pulled her headphones off from around her neck and put them aside. "It's not like you guys are officially dating or anything, right? So what's the worst that could happen? He doesn't want to see you anymore."

"He's a shifter and I still don't know what he can change into," I said dryly, "he could be capable of clawing my face off."

Ariana laughed. "This is Kane we're talking about. He's more likely to shift into something which can lick you to death. Besides, you have your gargoyle to protect you. Maybe two." She cocked her head. "You haven't seen the other one again, or the mysterious blur?"

"No." I had been watching for it for weeks now, but I hadn't noticed any more than a stray breeze, which I attributed to winter winds. Just thinking about them made me shiver. I peeled back my covers and slipped underneath them.

"I'm starting to think I was either imagining things, or someone was doing magic and I just happened to see some of it. The gargoyle was obviously from the same website we used in class. I should count myself lucky it didn't attack us."

Ariana nodded slowly. "That makes sense, I suppose. You wouldn't have been the first to use it."

"Exactly." I nodded. I felt better having figured all of that out. Now maybe I could put the sighting out of my mind and focus on more important things, like the guys—I mean, studying.

Even without sleeping with a lecturer, I was doing well. My mother would expect nothing less, naturally. Although I found the history of magic to be somewhat boring, I enjoyed learning about the anatomy of witches, wizards and shifters, loved defence training and even the psychology of para-normals. I still didn't know what I wanted to do when I had finished studying, but I had a lot of inter-esting options.

"Can I tell you something?" Ariana asked softly.

I glanced over at her. She looked nervous, as though she thought I wouldn't like whatever she had to say.

"Of course," I replied firmly. After all, we were friends and I had spent the last hour telling her about all of my dramas. Listening to her was the least I could do.

"I..." She blushed. "I'm bisexual." She bit her lip and looked worried.

"Oh," I said lightly, "that's great. You like guys and girls, right?"

"Right." She looked relieved. "You don't think I'm, I don't know, a freak or something?"

"Of course not, why would I?" I frowned at the idea that I'd judge her badly for something so natural.

"My parents are a bit funny about things like that," she admitted. "My siblings too. If they knew, they might not speak to me again."

"That's terrible," I blurted out. I slid out from under my warm blankets, sat beside her and took her hand. "I hope they would love you just the same as they do now, but if they don't, well, you have family here." Strange that for all my mother's short-comings, I didn't think she'd turn her back on me for my sexuality.

Ariana gave me a watery smile. "Really?"

"Absolutely," I said firmly. "You're my best friend here at the academy. I love you like a sister. I'm so glad we ended up roommates, even if you do snore."

She grinned. "I'm glad too. Although, I don't snore as much as you do."

"Do too," I said with a laugh. I drew her in for a quick hug.

"I love you too," she said in my ear, "like a sister. Although…"

I drew back and looked her in the eyes. "Although what?" I asked cautiously.

"If you were my sister, you would have put magic ants in my bed." She giggled.

"I could still do that," I offered. "Let me just get my phone."

"No thank you," she laughed. "It's a very tempting offer though."

I grinned. "All right. If you change your mind, you know where to find me." I stood and retreated back to my own bed. "You know what though?"

"What?" she asked.

"I wouldn't have put ants in your bed."

"No?"

"No. I would have put snakes. I prefer those to ants." I leaned back and pulled the blankets to my chin.

"Oh, so do I," she replied, "but not in my bed."

"I'll bear that in mind." I smiled.

She was silent for a while before she asked, "Reptiles or dicks?"

I snorted in surprise. "I beg your pardon?"

"Reptiles or dicks?" she asked again. "What kind of snakes would you put in my bed?"

"Ohhh." I pushed hair out of my eyes. "Which would you prefer?"

She looked thoughtful. "I guess that depends whether or not a guy was attached and how big the dick was."

"Substantial," I said with a nod. "A substantial cock, or a carpet snake."

"I think I'm going to have to go for the cock, as long as the guy attached is reasonably good looking."

"This is turning into one heck of a Christmas list," I joked. Christmas was half a year away and a hot guy was probably not on my list of obtainable items. At least, not ones I could give away. "Let's see, big cock, hot. Nice, I assume?"

"Definitely nice," she agreed. "I would also accept a hot girl with a strap-on."

I raised my eyebrow at that. "I'll make a note of that. A carpet snake might be easier. Or a dildo."

"I would never say no to a dildo." She lay on her side, facing me.

"A vibrator would be a lot less complicated than a relationship." My mind suddenly conjured up an image of Ariana using one on herself. Running it over her... I swallowed. Wasn't my life confusing enough, without throwing thoughts like that into the mix?

"If vibrators would make coffee, maybe we wouldn't need men," she joked.

I laughed. "They have their uses. Men, I mean."

"Yeah, but it would be great if dildos made coffee." She sighed.

"Yes," I agreed, "yes it would. Some day, maybe."

"Hey." She sat up suddenly. "Can we make coffee with magic?"

I frowned. "It's possible to heat water using magic, but I don't think we could conjure up a fresh cup. It would disappear like the magically created creatures."

"In that case, I'd rather conjure up cake. All the moistness and none of the calories." She lay back again.

"I think it would also have none of the taste of cake. That's probably why I've never heard of anyone doing it."

"It would make a good prank," she remarked. "If pranking was something either of us did."

"It would," I agreed. "Watch out for magic cake crumbs in your bed."

She laughed. "Now I know to wait until they disappear, I won't have to worry."

"Drat," I grumbled jokingly. "Now I'll have to think of something else." I clicked my fingers.

She giggled. "Can I ask you something?"

"Sure." I covered a yawn with my hand. "Fire away. So to speak."

"If you had to choose one guy, *only* one, who would you choose? Don't think too hard." She watched me over the top of her blankets.

I sighed. "I honestly don't know. I feel differently about them all, but I don't feel more for one than the others."

"I guess there's only one thing for it then," she said.

"Get a vibrator?" I suggested.

"Okay, there's only two things," she amended. "They'll have to fight it out in a duel."

I laughed. "To the death?"

"Oh no, nothing so savage," she said quickly. "Maybe just a friendly game of poker, or a joust."

I shook my head and laughed again. "As much fun as it would be to see them joust, I doubt it would end well."

Ariana pouted playfully. "I suppose not. I wonder who would win that though."

I mused for a moment. "Probably Nash. Kane

would hold back and... I don't know what Dyson would do."

"Maybe that's your answer," she said. "Nash is the only one who would fight for you."

"Physically fight, yes," I agreed. "But only in a joust. Dyson would win at poker. He gives away nothing about his thoughts. Nash's are all over his face."

"And Kane?"

I tucked my hair behind my ear. What would Kane excel at, apart from making me come in a garden full of people?

"I'm not sure," I said slowly, "herding naked brothers, perhaps?" As skills went, it was certainly an interesting one.

Ariana laughed. "Herding naked men could catch on, as an international sport."

"Indoor sport," I added. "A sunburnt dick would hurt like a bitch."

"Good point." She nodded. "Unless they were covered in sunblock. Just think how they'd all glisten then."

"I can totally imagine that. You should take the idea to the Olympic committee." I nestled into my pillow.

"Being naked at the Olympics is traditional," she said. "We could just go back to that."

"I suspect some of those family first groups might object," I said sleepily. "Won't someone think of the children?"

Ariana exhaled loudly out her nose. "You're right. Scratch that then. I guess you'll have to find something else he's good at."

"I will," I replied. It was possible whatever he shifted into was unique and allowed him to do something the others couldn't. Whatever that was. Wasn't Nash a shifter too? I had no idea what he could become. I would bet it's not a fluffy bunny or a kangaroo. No, nothing cute. Possibly a wolf or a lion.

I fell asleep imagining Nash as a wolf, with a long, nubile tongue.

18

"So what can you shift into?" I placed my plate and cup on the table and flopped down beside Kane.

He looked at me in surprise, a fork halfway to his mouth. Instead of lowering the utensil, he pushed the ravioli inside and started to chew. I suspected, to avoid having to answer my question.

That was okay, I could wait. I placed my arms on the table and sat patiently until he swallowed.

"Why?" he asked finally.

"Why what? Why do I want to know what you are?" I poked my own fork into my dinner. "Because you won't tell me, but that hasn't stopped me from wondering." In fact, I was more curious now than I was when I met him. What could be so bad that he wouldn't talk about it?

"Is it really that embarrassing?"

His face turned red.

That would be a yes, it was.

"You don't have to tell me, if you really don't want to," I said gently. "I'll contain my curiosity."

"No, I want to tell you," he said after a few moments when I thought he might get up and run. He sagged a little. "I'm a bird."

"Okay," I said slowly, "what kind?"

Kane put down his fork, placed his elbows on the table and propped his head on his hands. "An owl."

I blinked. "That's it?"

He sighed. "I know, it's underwhelming, isn't it?"

"I think it's amazing," I assured him. I was still confused though. "Why don't you want people to know about it?"

His brow creased. "Really? An owl, at a school of magic? Can you imagine how many people would ask me to carry letters for them?"

"Oh." I reached for his hand. "That would be annoying."

"Exactly. Dyson said he was going to write a letter and have me deliver it to everyone." He looked so sad my heart melted a little more.

"I'm sure he was joking," I said gently. "He might

be jealous he can't fly." I was. I would love to soar above the trees, to be free on the breeze.

Kane blinked a couple of times. "Do you think so?"

"Definitely. Being a dog is great and all but flying must be something really special." I squeezed his hand and gave him a smile.

"It really is," he enthused. "The world looks different from up there." He glanced toward the ceiling.

"Don't you have shifter training?" I asked before I released his hand and started eating.

He sagged again and averted his eyes. "I do private training. My trainer knows what I am, but he keeps it quiet."

"He?" I asked.

"Yeah, Nash." Kane stuck a fork in a piece of ravioli.

"Ah." My face heated. "So you know him pretty well then?"

Kane shrugged. "Well enough, I suppose. Not enough to know what he can shift into. Why?"

I almost responded by saying, "No reason," but I didn't want to lie. "I…" I swallowed hard. "We have a thing. I don't exactly know what it is or where it'll go, but—"

"A thing?" Kane echoed. He didn't seem to be angry or upset, just surprised.

"Yeah, um." How did I put this? "Sex."

"Ah." He nodded, then cocked his head. "Does this mean you don't want to see me anymore?" Anxiety flashed through his eyes.

"No, I still want to. If you want to?" Now I was the anxious one.

"I do want to," he said quickly. "I like you. A lot. More than a lot." He blushed. "If you want to see other guys too, that's up to you. I hope you choose me in the long run though." I didn't think it was possible, but his blush deepened. He was just so stinking adorable.

I leaned over to kiss his mouth.

His arm went around my neck to draw me in closer and deepen the kiss. He broke off just before I became completely breathless.

"Peyton and Kane, sitting in a tree," he said, smiling at his rendition of the children's rhyme. "K-i-s-s-i-n-g."

"Not unless you can fly us both up there," I pointed out. "Or if it's not too high up."

"I'll bring a ladder," he said with a smile. "As long as I get to kiss you."

"I'm all for keeping my feet on the ground, but I

like the kissing part." I leaned in for another.

"Do I have to throw a bucket of water over you both?" Dyson asked. He slipped into the chair opposite his brother.

"Do you have one?" I asked teasingly.

He grinned. "I'm sure I could find one."

I stuck out my tongue at him. Was he jealous? I couldn't see anything in his eyes but humour. He was the kind of guy, I decided, who hid his feelings behind jokes. I liked to laugh as much as the next person, but I wanted to know what was going on with him. He was a closed book, or a closed phone with a complicated passcode.

"There are better ways to make me wet," I told him, trying to get some kind of response.

"I bet there are." His eyes travelled down my body. "Although that kiss looked it would have done that already."

"I…" He wasn't wrong about that.

"I'm going to get another drink," Kane said suddenly. "Do you want anything?"

I waved toward my untouched glass of cola. "No thanks, I'm good for now."

Kane nodded, gave me a meaningful look and hurried away.

"Well, that was subtle," Dyson said sarcastically.

"Oh, you thought so too, huh?" I grimaced. "I think he's suggesting I talk to you about…things."

"Things? I'm always up for a discussion about things. What kind of things? Dicks?" He grinned, but his eyes seemed guarded. "I could go on about mine all day."

I smiled. "I'm sure you could. I mean… What do you *want* to do with it? With me. If anything," I added in a hurry. "I mean…" The words stuck in my throat. A frank conversation had quickly become awkward, especially since he just sat there watching me make a fool of myself.

"Do I want to sleep with you?" he said finally.

"Yes. No." I took a sip of cola to wet my mouth. "We went on a date. We had fun, didn't we? And we've had fun since."

"Ah." He nodded. "Is this about you inviting me into your room and me saying no?"

"Yes." That was exactly what this was about. "Was it something I said or did?"

He licked his lips. "No, not at all. It's nothing like that."

"Then, what is it like?" I asked before I could stop myself.

"This is going to sound strange," he said slowly. "I walk around naked and talk about my dick, but when it comes to relationships, I like to take it slowly."

"Oh." Now I felt silly. I had jumped to all kinds of conclusions, but never to this. "You mean... Just because you're naked, doesn't mean you're asking for it?"

"Pretty much." He gave me a lopsided smile. "Is that weird?"

"No, not at all. Women have been telling men that since forever. I should have realised it goes both ways. I'm sorry." I looked toward my half-empty plate.

"You're forgiven." He put a finger under my chin and turned my face toward him. "I like you, a lot. I'm used to being the jokester. Talking about my feelings is difficult, but I'll try." He gave me a look of warmth that made my heart skip a beat.

"You're doing great," I said softly. "I like you too."

He lowered his hand and leaned over to kiss me softly on my lips before he sat back. "I'm very likeable." The jokester was back now, but I had seen enough of his tender side to satisfy me.

"Yes, you are." I patted his cheek.

"When you're not being annoying." Kane sat back in his chair and looked from his brother to me and back again.

"When am I ever annoying?" Dyson gave us both a look of pure innocence.

Kane snorted.

I wondered what it would be like to have them naked and sweaty, on either side of me, lips, tongues, hands... I sipped my cola to cover the expression on my face. I probably had lust written all over it.

"You're both wonderful," I said when I could trust myself to talk. "In your own unique ways."

Dyson grinned. "He told you what he could shift into, didn't he?"

"I did," Kane muttered.

"I think it's great," I said firmly. "I was worried it would be a chihuahua or a camel."

Dyson threw back his head and laughed. "I've never heard of a camel shifter."

"Of course you haven't," I said, "who would admit to being one?"

Kane was grinning now. "Maybe that's what Nash is."

I shook my head and laughed. "I can't picture it, somehow. He'd be more likely to be a wolf." I thought back to my dream and licked my lips.

"If he was a wolf, the whole academy would know about it," Kane pointed out. "No one would want to hide it if they were one. Same with lions, tigers and bears."

"Oh my," Dyson added.

"That's true," I agreed. To be honest, I wouldn't rule out the idea that he was the gargoyle, but I didn't say it out loud. I'd sooner accept my assumption that someone had created it and I'd just been in the right place to catch a glimpse.

"So, you and Nash too, huh?" Dyson asked, his tone blunt but his expression still jovial.

"Yeah." I explained the situation to him as I had done with Kane.

Dyson nodded. "Got it. Three guys vying for your heart. May the best paranormal win." He winked at me. "I look forward to that being me."

"Dream on," Kane told him. He shot his brother a scowl.

Dyson responded with a smile.

Kane did have a head start on his brother, but I wouldn't assume anything at this point. For all I knew, it might not work out with any of them. If that was the case, I would be disappointed, but I'd accept it. Love was one of those things in life you couldn't force, no matter how much you might want to.

Wait, did I just say love? I liked these guys, but I

wasn't there yet. Some day, maybe. The problem was, I could see myself falling head over heels for all of them. At some point, I would have to decide who I liked the best. I didn't want to think about that day. It might be that by then one or two would have drifted away and gotten involved with other people. It might also be that they didn't and I would have to hurt someone.

Gods, complicated suddenly seemed like one hells of an understatement.

"So, Peyton, would you like to see a movie after dinner?" Kane asked.

"I'd love to," I agreed.

"So, Peyton, would you like to go out with me tomorrow night?" Dyson asked.

"I'd love to do that too," I replied.

"Game on, brother," Dyson grinned.

Kane rolled his eyes. "This isn't a game."

"No, I suppose not." Dyson looked serious for a change. "That doesn't mean I'm not going to walk away with Peyton on my arm at the end of it."

"If you guys are going to fight over me..." I said in warning. "If this comes between you, I'm done. With both of you. I'm not going to create problems between brothers."

"You won't," Dyson assured me. "This is how we usually are."

"It really is," Kane agreed.

I hesitated. "Well, good then." The last thing I wanted was to start a war between them. I sensed their brotherly bond was fragile enough. I refused to be the one who broke it.

19

"WHAT THE FUCK?" I stopped dead in my tracks. I hadn't seen any gargoyles, apart from the one on my arm, for weeks. The site we used in class had removed the option, but Madame Luc hadn't offered any explanation for why it was there in the first place.

I hadn't called up the one on my arm either. To be honest, the idea of doing that scared me. What if it didn't work? What if it did work and the creature turned on me? It might hurt someone else it wasn't supposed to. The list of what might go wrong went on, but those were my top three.

Imagine my surprise then, to see one in front of me on the sidewalk on my way back from a morning run. Spring was in the air today, but only a hint of it.

Winter's fingers still gripped the city. Before too long, we'd be bitching about the heat and preparing for Christmas.

Right now though, my attention was on the creature in front of me. Long hind legs, shorter front ones, long, wide ears, horns. It looked just like my tattoo. Or vice versa.

Like a cat, it stepped toward me, red eyes focused firmly on my face.

I raised my hands. "I'm harmless, honest." I swallowed and took a step back.

The gargoyle moved forward, to cover the space between us. He—for some reason I thought that was the right pronoun—bared his teeth at me.

"I don't taste good either," I said. Although given Kane had spent most of the last three movies we'd been to with his face buried between my legs, maybe that wasn't accurate. I wasn't planning to offer the creature a taste of my sex.

The gargoyle snorted softly, as though it found my words amusing.

That was weird.

"Wait, you can understand me?" The magically created one had given no sign of having understood a word. It was—for want of a better expression—a mindless killing machine. This was something different.

"You're a shifter, aren't you?" I lowered my arms and crossed them over my chest. I was still somewhat cautious, but no longer scared. I could deal with a shifter if I had to. Maybe. Okay, I *hoped* I could.

The gargoyle cocked its head at me and let out a low growl.

"Nope," I said without flinching. "I'm not buying it. Try again."

He sniffed as though trying harder was beneath him somehow. In spite of that, he snapped at me. His teeth came to within a centimetre of my leg.

I jumped back a little. "Hey, watch it!" I swear to the gods the gargoyle laughed at me. The sound came from the back of his throat and was only slightly less intimidating than his growl.

"You're an asshole, you know that?" I told him.

He licked his muzzle in response.

"Yeah, whatever." I rolled my eyes. "Why are you following me? This is the third time I've seen you. Unless there are two others like you out there."

For some reason, that seemed to infuriate him. He growled again, deeper this time, but I sensed it wasn't directed at me. He was angry at the implications of what I'd said, not because I'd said it.

"You don't like the idea there might be others like you?" I asked. "Why? Do you want to be special or something?"

He raised a clawed foot and waved it at me.

I exhaled. "This would be a lot easier if you shifted and talked to me like an actual person." I squinted at him. "Nash, is that you? I'm not going to be upset that you're a gargoyle, or if you've been following me. Promise."

The gargoyle snorted loudly.

Not Nash. Thank goodness I didn't say anything more provocative.

"Okay, can we clear up one thing," I said. "Have you been following me? Nod for yes."

Nod.

"All right, now we're getting somewhere. Can you tell me why?"

Head shake.

"Am I in danger of some kind?"

Nod.

"Wonderful," I said sarcastically. "From you?"

Head shake.

"That's good to know." I put a finger to my lips. "Is this about my mother?"

The gargoyle disappeared. Don't get me wrong, this is a reasonable response to any mention of my mother. I've wished many times that I could do exactly that. In this case, it was beyond irritating, and it was strange. The creature didn't lope away into the night, it was just...gone.

"I'm well acquainted with the trick of forming a bubble around oneself and becoming invisible," I said dryly. What I had never seen, or heard of, was a shifter with magic. "Come on, drop that thing and let's talk."

Footsteps moved away from me; the scratching of long claws on pavement. The gargoyle was leaving. Although a magic bubble hid a witch or wizard from the eye, it didn't hide sound. Dude was a mani-pedi away from creeping off, but it was enough that I couldn't guess what direction he was heading.

"Wait a minute," I called after it. "Come back tell me what the hells is going on. Please."

Unfortunately, the sun had risen a while ago, and people started to step out of their homes and head to work. Several gave me a funny look as they hurried past. Not as funny as the one they would have given to the gargoyle, but bad enough. Hells, this was Sydney, surely they'd seen worse than a person talking to themselves on an otherwise quiet street?

I shot them a smile and brushed my hair off my face. Whatever was going on, I wasn't going to find out right now. Stupid gargoyle. What was the point of following me and warning me, but not telling me what I should be looking out for? Very helpful. Not.

I shook my head and started back toward the academy at a slow jog. I would get to the bottom of this, one way or another. In fact, I knew just the person to ask.

"How can a gargoyle shifter do magic?" I planted my hands on my hips and gave Nash a direct look. If anyone would have the answers, it would be him. I wasn't leaving until he did.

He closed the door behind me and locked it.

I had been to his room before. The space was clean and tidy, almost too much so. It looked almost un-lived in. I knew that wasn't true, he was just a clean freak. I had seen him straighten out chairs and bedsheets until they were exactly how he wanted them. Nothing was out of place now. I bet even dust didn't dare to venture into here.

I returned my gaze to him and arched an eyebrow.

He sighed and gestured for me to sit on one of the plump armchairs to the side of the room.

"It's a long story," he started.

"I have time," I said.

He sat down in the chair beside mine but perched on the edge as though he couldn't relax while talking about this. Whatever *this* was.

He scratched his head. "They can do magic because they're hybrids."

"Come again?" I asked.

"I'd love to." He looked weary but managed a smile. "I think that will have to wait until after this."

"Damn right," I said. "So what the fuck do you mean by hybrid? I know witches and shifters can breed, but the kids are one or the other."

He nodded. "That's right. Or at least, it was." He blew out a long breath through pursed lips.

When he didn't go on, I waved a hand at him. "It was until what?"

He sat back in the chair and steepled his fingers. "Until Zeta started blending witch and shifter DNA. They created hybrids with what they deemed the ideal mix of magics."

"Wait, back up a bit." I leaned forward and put my hands on my knees. "Zeta? What's that?"

He rubbed the tip of his nose. "They're a government department. More or less top secret. Definitely evil. They're committed to bringing the world under their heel, with the help of their hybrids. They want to kill off the rest of the paranormals."

"Well that sucks," I said dryly. "So wait, they're taking bits of two kinds of paranormals and making a whole new breed?" My mind twisted and turned with that information. How could that even be possible? It seemed like something out of a science fiction book.

"Exactly." Nash nodded.

"And the gargoyle is a hybrid?" A created being, not unlike the one I had had tattooed on my arm. How was that for irony?

"More than likely," he agreed. "Zeta apparently has a twisted sense of humour, because all of their hybrids are creatures from mythology."

"That certainly explains the gargoyle," I agreed. "So there's others out there? Sphinxes? Unicorns?" I thought about the one on Ariana's arm. This was going to blow her mind.

"Possibly, although I haven't met any of those in particular."

"So, how do you know all of this?" I asked.

He cleared his throat. "Because I'm a hybrid."

My mouth dropped open. "Are you a gargoyle too?"

He snorted. "No." He looked away, toward the window. "I'm a dragon."

I blinked and stared at him. "No shit?"

He looked back at me, a faint smile on his lips. "No shit. I can also do magic."

I shook my head to try to clear it. "That's why you don't need a tattoo," I guessed. "Because you're already your own badass protector."

He smiled faintly. "Something like that. I try not to let the dragon loose though. Things don't...end well."

I reached over to put my hand on his. "This—Zeta—they did things to you, didn't they?" I kept my tone gentle. Not only because I cared about him, but because no smart person pisses a dragon off.

He shifted uncomfortably. "I used to work for them. A long time ago, before I knew..." he shook his head. "I helped them to do some terrible things."

"But then you stopped," I said.

He smiled faintly. "Yes. They didn't like it much."

I frowned. "That's why you had to take a life? Did they come after you?"

"Me and some friends," he said, his voice a harsh

whisper. His eyes looked haunted. He must be thinking back to that moment.

I chewed at my lip. "It sounds a bit like they deserved it." I knew that was a terrible thing to say, but there were some awful people in the world. Now there was a few less. Maybe I was more like my mother than I'd realised. Ugh, that sucked.

"Just because someone is an evil asshole, doesn't mean they deserve to die," he said without irony.

"I beg to differ," I said dryly, "but it's done now and I won't judge you for it." He wouldn't have done it if he'd had another option, I knew that with everything inside me. "What happened to your friends?"

He shrugged with a shoulder. "They're probably still out there, fighting back. Zeta knew me too well, so I'm here. New identity and all."

"Oh really?" I asked, "what were you before?"

He smiled wryly. "I was a cop."

I nodded. "I can see you doing that. Helping people and all."

He snorted. "Yeah, maybe a little, here and there." He paused before he added, "My name used to be Richard."

I grinned. "Dick?"

He rolled his eyes. "Yeah, I got that from time to time. Now, is it time for you to get some dick?"

I stood and pulled him to his feet. "I think it's past time."

He let my hand go and swept off my shirt before he guided me to the bed and the scarves draped over the end. He tied my wrists firmly and started a long, slow exploration of my body.

20

IT WASN'T until much later I realised I hadn't asked Nash why a shifter might be following me. On the other hand, the whole Zeta things was more or less explanatory. They sounded like exactly the kind of people my mother would butt heads with.

Unless…

My breath caught in my throat. If Nash had worked with them, maybe she had too. She had always been vocal about the superiority of paranormals over normal people. To think she would work an organisation Nash described as evil—surely even she wouldn't go that far?

"Hey, is your hearing switched off or your brain?"

I blinked, surprised to see Matt standing in front

of me. Outside the academy was a public place, but that didn't explain why he'd talk to me.

"Gargoyle got your tongue?" he asked derisively.

I shook my head slightly. "I beg your pardon?" Had he just said what I thought he'd said? How the hells did he know about that?

"Gargoyle." He pointed toward my arm. "Or have you forgotten you got inked already?"

Oh. Duh. I narrowed my eyes at him. "Fuck off, Matt."

He grinned. "Great comeback." He started to clap slowly, sarcastically.

"Yeah, whatever." I rolled my eyes. "Did you want something?"

"Not particularly." He smirked. "You just looked like you'd seen a ghost."

"Would you care if I had?" I asked.

"I might not like you, but I have some compassion for my fellow paranormals." He leaned against the wall beside us and crossed his arms over his chest.

I tried to ignore how his muscles bulged out of his black t-shirt. Did he ever wear any other colour? "Right." I exhaled through pursed lips. "I'm fine. Thanks for asking."

"Are you sure?" He lowered his chin and looked at me under his brows.

"Yeah." I couldn't exactly confide in him, could I? "I just got some news. I'm trying to process it."

"Bad news?" he asked.

"I'm not sure," I admitted. "It's complicated."

"Do you want to talk about it?" He quirked an eyebrow at me.

"I thought you didn't like me?" I mimicked his expression.

"I don't, but I'm not a complete dick. If someone needs to get something off their chest, I can listen."

"As tempting as that is," and it was, a little bit, "I'm not sure what there is to say. I need to think about things for a while." And I really needed to talk to Kane and Dyson. If anyone would know about hybrids…okay, they might know nothing, but they deserved to know.

He pushed himself off the wall. "Suit yourself. Just do me a favour and be careful, all right? I've heard some strange rumours about something going down in the paranormal world."

Now he had my attention. "What kind of rumours?"

He ran a hand over his hair. "I'm not exactly sure. Just…strange ones."

"Is it about Zeta?" The words were out before I could stop them.

His lips dropped apart. "How do you know about them?" he asked carefully.

"From a friend," I replied as casually as I could. "How do *you* know about them?"

His expression shut down hard. His eyes were like chips of stone. No hint of emotion was visible in their depths.

"If I were you, I'd stay well away from them and don't mention them again," he said coldly.

"And what if I do?" I stood my ground. I wasn't scared of him, nor would I let him intimidate me.

He hesitated for a moment, then with some effort relaxed his pose. "Then it's your funeral, I guess. If you're lucky."

I cocked my head. "What do you mean by that?"

He leaned in until his nose was almost touching mine. "I mean Zeta likes to use paranormals for their own gain. They won't wait around until you give permission for it either."

I tried not to flinch, but I thought back to what Nash had said about the creation of hybrids. Someone had to carry those children and supply the DNA. The only way either of those things would happen would be against my will.

I swallowed and took a step back. I forced a smile as though not completely rattled by all of this. "Why aren't we fighting back?"

"Who says we aren't?" he asked. "Do you think students would be privy to that kind of information?"

"Apparently you are," I said ironically.

He shrugged. "I made it a point to find out, after..." he shook his head. "It doesn't matter. The point is, you're better off to keep your pretty little nose out of all of this."

"Too late," I replied simply. "I'm not letting this go, just because you think I should." Especially if he was going to be so condescending.

"Don't think I'll weep at your funeral," he said.

"I'm surprised you'd even be there," I retorted.

Something flashed across his face, something like regret. It was gone before I could do more than register it. "You're right," he admitted. "I have something more important to do that day."

"You're a real fucking charmer, you know that?" I said sarcastically.

He grinned. "Of course I am. When I like someone."

"For your information, I'm very likeable," I said with a sniff.

"You're fuckable, but that's about it," he said coolly.

"Wow, what a compliment." I snorted. "It would be a cold day in all the hells before I let you go there."

"You seem to be busy enough as it is," he replied. "Do your knees even recognise each other?"

My mouth dropped open. "Did you just try to slut shame me?"

He shrugged one shoulder. "If the hat fits…"

Before I could think, I held out my palm, formed a ball of magic and hurled it at him. It struck him in the middle of his oh-so-chiseled chest and knocked him back off his feet. He landed on his ass with a grunt of pain.

He leapt up with a growl and tossed a ball of magic back at me.

I ducked sideways. It soared past my shoulder and slammed into a tree, sending bark flying in every direction.

"Really?" I asked angrily. "Mine wasn't made to do that much damage."

He shrugged and made another ball of magic. "I wasn't aiming to kill. That time." He drew back his hand, his eyes fixed on mine.

A thrill of fear passed down my spine. Without thinking, I dropped to a crouch and threw myself at his legs. He went down again, hard. The ball of magic went wide. It hit an electrical pole and sent up a shower of sparks.

"You fucking idiot." I rolled off him. "Are you trying to kill us all?" Just in case, I formed another ball of magic.

He stood on unsteady legs. "Not all of us, no."

"Just me?" I watched him carefully for any sign of his next move.

"You threw the first shot," he pointed out.

"Only because you were being an asshole," I retorted.

"I was not, I was just being honest." He stood straight, hands at his sides.

"That's one way to put it. I stand by my assessment of you—you're an asshole."

He grinned. "You're only saying that because you don't know me."

"Thank the gods for that," I said. "You're probably worse than an asshole." I decided he wasn't going to attack me again and let the magic dissipate, but I remained on my guard.

His mouth quirked to the side. "What's worse than that?"

"I don't know and I don't really care." Whatever it was, it could stay away from me.

"Of course you don't, you're too busy messing around in things you shouldn't be, and throwing magic at people who aren't your enemy."

"Says you," I told him. "You're doing a pretty good imitation of an enemy as far as I can see."

He raised his chin and barked a laugh. "If you think that, you must have had a much more sheltered life than I guessed. Compared to some, I'm completely harmless." His eyes shone with amusement and condescension. What a dick. He knew nothing about me, except that I had a tattoo and was involved with Kane. How dare he correctly assume my life had been sheltered up until now?

Rude!

I purpose my lips. "You're referring to Zeta again?" I guessed. "For someone who thinks I should forget about them, you bring them up a lot." I cocked my head in what I hoped was a challenging look.

He blew out a frustrated breath. "I didn't say you should forget. I said you should be careful and not get involved. Or complacent. It's likely they have agents here at the academy. They're probably on the look out for their latest victims."

Part of me wanted to laugh and accuse him of being melodramatic. Instead, a shiver went down my spine. The idea that anyone at the academy would sell us out to an evil government organisation was nothing less than horrifying. Who would do such a thing?

My mouth went dry. How about someone who worked with them? Nash claimed he didn't anymore, but what if that wasn't the truth? What if his desire to dominate me went beyond sex?

"I see it's finally sinking in," Matt said. "Don't trust anyone."

"Including you?" I asked.

"Especially me," he agreed. "You don't know me from the next guy."

"And you're shifty as fuck," I added.

He laughed. "That too. At least I'm hot."

I rolled my eyes. "That's a matter of opinion." If he wasn't such a dick, I would tear his clothes off and screw him silly. Damn it. I didn't want to think that way about him. He was infuriating.

"I can see that opinion on your face." He was so smug I almost sent another ball of magic at him, this time at his head.

I grunted. "You suck at reading people."

"No I don't." He shook his head. "I'm very good at it. In fact—" He stopped and his eyes widened. He came toward me at a run and slammed me down to the ground.

I landed with a thud, the wind knocked out of me. How I didn't hit my head on the concrete and break it open, I didn't know. Still, everything was going to hurt like a bitch later.

What the fuck?

A snapping sound, followed by an angry shriek echoed across the area.

"What the fuck?" I asked when my breath returned.

"Shut up and stay down."

As if I had a choice. His body lay on top of mine, his arms over my head. I was pinned down hard.

Something big soared over the top of us. It turned and headed back.

"Shit. Shit, shit shit. Don't move." Matt buried his face in my shoulder and froze.

I bit back a cry of alarm as a winged creature passed overhead. For a moment, I thought maybe it was a dragon. Then I got a clear look and my heart raced like a drumroll. Great gods above, it couldn't be. Could it?

The phoenix was huge—twice as big as a grown person—and covered from head to toe in bright blue feathers. At the shoulder, they were midnight blue. The shade lightened down the wings, to a brilliant blue at the ends. The phoenix might be pretty if it wasn't obviously hells bent on attacking us. The creature let out a long, low shriek and circled above us. They made a dive and snapped with the enormous beak.

"I think they can see us," I said, my voice high. "Get off me so I can throw some magic at them."

"No," Matt growled. "I'm going to roll off. When I do that, you're going to run. Get inside the academy and close the door."

"I'm not just going to run," I argued.

"Then you'll die," he snapped. "On three. One. Two. Three." He rolled away.

INSTEAD OF JUMPING up and running, I leapt to my feet and aimed a ball of magic at the phoenix.

When it came over for another pass, I drew back my arm and waited. Just a bit closer, just a bit...

"Peyton, no!"

Matt's shout registered a fraction of a second after I released the ball of magic. Let's face it, I wouldn't have listened to him anyway. Hey, I never said I made the best choices.

The ball struck the phoenix on its face. It shimmered against the blue feathers for a moment, then grew and came back at me twice the size of the one I'd sent.

"Fuck!" I threw up a bubble of magic around me. The ball hit a heartbeat later and sizzled. I gritted my teeth to hold the magic in place. If it gave out, I was done for.

Blood pounded in my ears, raced around my body, a hot torrent of adrenaline. The bubble started to fail.

For the first time since I'd seen the phoenix, I was truly scared.

Matt called out something, but I couldn't make it out. A moment later, there he was, beside me, reinforcing the bubble with his own magic.

I let out a sob of relief as the pressure was shared, then lessened. The ball of magic gradually lost its power. No, Matt was absorbing it into our bubble. Whatever, we'd live to fight another minute or two.

"What part of "get inside" did you not understand?" he growled.

"The part where you don't get to tell me what to do," I retorted.

"And look where that got you," he snapped. "It almost got you killed."

"I was taking care of it." I glanced around. Where was the phoenix anyway, and how the hells had it amplified my magic like that?

"Bullshit. Another second or two and you'd be dead." He too was looking around.

"Yeah, well, thanks. Why is this fucker trying to kill me anyway?"

"Maybe he knows how annoying you are," Matt replied.

"How do you know it's a he?" I decided to ignore the insult, since he had—you know—saved my life.

"Just a guess." He turned in a circle, eyes skyward.

"Do you think he's gone?" I asked. I caught sight of faces peering out the window at us. Yeah, thanks for the help everyone.

"Not a chance. He won't have given up that easily." Matt sounded troubled. "We need to get insi —duck!"

For once I had the sense to listen. I dropped to a crouch as the phoenix made another pass. He opened his beak and scooped up a mouthful of magic as he went.

"What the hells?" I stared.

Matt pulled me to my feet and gave me a shove toward the academy door. "Get inside, *now*."

I staggered toward the threshold and turned. "What are you going to—"

My mouth dropped open as Matt stopped still and shifted. Yes, you guessed it, into a gargoyle. All right, in retrospect I should have figured it out, but I hadn't. Yet there he was, horns and all. His skin—or was that hide—was a glistening black, his eyes orange and red, like flame.

He let out a deep growl.

The phoenix shrieked in response.

I clapped my hands over my ears and stepped back further into the building.

"Peyton, what the hells is going on?"

I turned my head at the sound of Kane's voice. He and Dyson hurried down the corridor toward me. The whole academy administration peered through the door at me. At least three quarters of the students gathered around the windows, all trying to catch a glimpse.

"Just a little phoenix attack," I said as lightly as I could.

Kane put his arms around me and drew me to him.

Dyson looked a little pale. "Phoenix?"

I nodded. "The gargoyle is on our side. I think."

The phoenix screeched and flew at Matt. In the middle of the street, they slammed into each other. The phoenix grabbed a hold of Matt's arm, uh, leg, with his beak. He tugged his head to the side and grazed his beak down the bone of Matt's leg.

Matt let out a scream of pain. He tried to jerk his leg free, but his opponent held tight. His back legs scrabbled fast and hard, to keep him upright. I sensed if he fell, he was dead.

"What do we do?" I asked frantically. "Magic bounces off him."

"I don't think an owl is much of a match for that," Kane said quietly.

"Neither is a dog," Dyson replied. He sighed loudly.

I grabbed out my phone and clicked on the app. "There must be something." I scrolled down the menu of creatures and dismissed them as I went. The magpie was too small. The goat was—well—a goat. Cat, dingo, fox, horse, zebra. Crap, that was it.

I almost threw my phone against the wall in frustration. What good was learning all of this if we were helpless during one attack?

The invader forced Matt down lower and lower. Matt snapped at him and writhed, but he was getting increasingly weaker.

Finally his legs gave out and he fell to the road. His attacker stood over him, wings outspread, legs to either side of him. He let out a shriek of victory that threatened to shred every nerve in my body. His head snaked back and forth, then he opened his beak. I was sure he was about to rip out Matt's throat.

"Fuck this," I growled. I put my phone away and ran out toward the road.

"Peyton, no!" Kane called out behind me.

"Hey, fucker!" I waved my arms in the air. "It's me you want, right? Well, here I am. Come and get me."

The phoenix turned slowly, then stepped off Matt. His gaze was intent on me.

"Good boy," I taunted. "You don't want to kill anyone, right? Well, anyone but me. I don't suppose you can tell me why?"

The phoenix moved toward me, slow and deliberate. He was hunting me.

"I guess not." I shrugged. My hands sweated like crazy and I felt sick. At any moment, the phoenix would lunge and it would be all over for me. Fine, whatever, as long as no one else got hurt.

"You all right, Matt?" I called around the phoenix.

He groaned, shifted back into human form and crawled behind a parked car. In the corner of my eye, I saw Dyson and Kane run out to help him back inside.

"It's just you and me then, fucker," I told the phoenix. "What have you got?" Okay, it was a dumb question, but let's face it, I knew the answer. He was a shifter with magic. Not just magic, but the power to expand and deflect the magic of others. Created, I assume, by Zeta in some kind of laboratory. Just like Matt and Nash. Gods, who else was a hybrid around here?

The phoenix stepped toward me, his beak open, tongue licking the air between us.

"You have disgusting breath," I told him. If he could amplify magic, I wonder…

I pulled back my sleeve to expose my tattoo.

The phoenix's eyes narrowed. Uh-ha, he knew what I was up to. Before he could move away, I flicked my arm and willed my personal gargoyle to come to life. With a rush of air, the magic flew toward the phoenix and hit him on the wing.

A moment later a shape formed on the road between us. The gargoyle was twice the size of the one I had created in class. Twice the size of Matt. It growled deeply.

The phoenix backed up a few steps.

"Peyton!"

I registered Nash's presence a moment before he rushed out onto the road and stood beside me.

"Are you going to tell me to go inside, sir?" I eyed him in my peripheral vision.

"You seem to have this under control," he said. "Nice work."

"Thank you, sir. It's good to have you out here

with me though." I figured there was no safer place to be than shoulder to shoulder with a dragon.

"I wouldn't be anywhere else," he said. "Sorry it took so long though. I didn't know this was happening until Ariana told me."

I frowned. "Ariana, where is she?" I realised I hadn't seen her in any of this.

"Inside," Nash said simply. "Safe. Luckily she knew who to come to."

"How—" The question would have to wait for another time. The gargoyle lunged at the phoenix and raked its claws down a wing. It drew back for another attack, but promptly disappeared. Just as well, it could have inflicted a lot more damage at its present size. As it was, it had done enough.

The phoenix shrieked and tried to flap, but the wing dangled helplessly. Frantic, it backed up a handful of steps and desperately flapped its other wing. It lifted off the ground half a metre but flopped back down again.

He let out a pitiful creel and tucked his good wing to his back.

"Is that a surrender?" I asked.

"Possibly." Nash sounded troubled. He took a few tentative steps forward, hands out in front of him.

"Give it up," he told the phoenix. "It's over now. You can escape here."

The phoenix lowered his head and gave another creel, this one even sadder than the first.

I almost felt sorry for him, but he had tried to kill me.

"Shift," Nash ordered. "Let's see who you really are."

The phoenix's head wove back and forth on his neck. I took that as a no. That was understandable. We paranormals spent our lives trying to hide our secret identities from the world. Even assassin phoenixes. Especially them, probably.

"You can shift alive and answer my questions, or you can do it dead," Nash said. "Frankly, I don't care which." His tone was so cold it made me shiver. He meant every word. I doubted anyone there thought otherwise.

"I'd prefer alive," I said, "then I'd know why this was happening."

Nash glanced over his shoulder at me.

That was all the distraction the phoenix needed. He snapped out his supposedly damaged wing and took flight.

"Shit!" Nash cursed.

For a moment I thought he might shift and give

chase. Instead, he turned back and ushered me inside. In a matter of moments, the phoenix was gone.

"What the hells was that?" I asked. "I've never seen magic heal so quickly."

"Hybrid," was all Nash said. "If they came after you, they'll try again. It's unlikely they'll wait too long."

"Why me?" I demanded. "What did I do to Zeta?"

"It's probably not about what you did," Nash replied, "but what you could do for them."

"Which is what?" I asked. "I'm just an ordinary witch."

Nash gave me a long look. "To be honest, I don't know. There's something about you they want and they won't stop until they get it."

"Well that's fucking great," I muttered. "At least they don't want me dead."

His mouth set in a firm line. "Whatever they need, you might wish they had killed you before they take it."

"That's reassuring," I said dryly.

"It isn't meant to be," he said simply. "Get your friends and lovers and meet me in the training room. It's time we all had a little talk."

That sounded ominous. "All right. Sir."

He shot me look that made my blood heat. The adrenaline surge was gone, but it hadn't diminished his ability to arouse me with only a glance. Damn the man, he knew it too.

"Don't take long." He gave my hand a quick squeeze. "I'll be keeping a closer eye on you from now on." He leaned in to whisper in my ear. "Maybe I should just keep you tied up, for your own good."

My knees weak, I hurried off to find Kane and Dyson.

2 2

I FLOPPED down onto the soft training floor between Kane and Dyson. Matt sat opposite me, dressed in clean clothes, apparently healed after almost having a leg chewed off. Ariana sat beside him, her head lowered, hair over part of her face. Nash paced.

I followed him with my eyes.

"Can we start with why Zeta wants me dead?" I said. I had considered asking why the hells Matt was here in the first place, but he had defended me. That was another question I wanted answers for, but it wasn't as important as the one I had asked.

Nash stopped pacing and waved a hand toward Ariana. "I think she can answer that."

I gaped at Ariana, who raised her head and swallowed visibly. Her face was pale. She looked…scared.

"She can?" I asked, confused. I fixed my gaze on her. "You can?"

"Can I just begin by saying I didn't mean to deceive you. I mean, I did, but—" She ran a hand over her hair.

My heart sank. "You're working with them?"

Kane growled and moved as if to rise and throw himself at her.

I put out an arm to hold him back. "Let's hear her out first."

Ariana licked her lips. "I don't work for Zeta, no. I work with—" She glanced toward Nash. "Factors who are fighting back against them. Your mother…"

"What about her? Is she working with Zeta?" I snapped. I was getting tired of these half answers.

"She used to," Ariana said, her voice small.

I leaned back and looked toward the ceiling to compose myself. "She doesn't now?"

"It's hard to break ties with them," Ariana said slowly.

Nash snorted. "She's right there. Your mother is too high profile to hide." He didn't need to add, "Like I did." The words hung in the air.

"What did she do for them?" I wasn't sure I wanted the answer to that, but I needed to know.

"She…" Ariana chewed her lip. "Zeta was trying

to incorporate paranormal DNA with that of normals. To do that, they needed test subjects."

My stomach turned. "Please don't tell me she supplied those test subjects."

Ariana looked away.

"Oh gods." I was going to throw up all over the perfectly good training floor.

Kane put an arm around me, and I leaned into him. Gods knew I was no fan of my mother, but I had no idea she was such a monster. That left so many questions about my own conception and development, but I didn't want to think about that, not yet.

Once my head stopped spinning, the implications hit me like a blow to the face. I don't mean a blow job, I mean the bad kind.

"You knew about this?" I pulled away from Kane and glanced around the room.

"I knew," Ariana said quickly. "I was sent here to keep an eye on you. To keep you safe."

I narrowed my eyes at her. "So, you're not new to magic?"

"That part is true," she said. "My aunt Chrissy works with—I guess you could call them the resistance. She thought I'd be less obvious than someone who is a known shifter." She nodded toward Matt.

"Right." I turned to Matt. "Where do you fit into all of this?"

He shrugged. "Same. I was asked to keep an eye on you. I argued against it, on the grounds you're a spoilt brat, but they insisted."

I snorted. "Gee, thanks."

He smirked. "You're welcome. And don't thank me for saving your ass."

"As I recall, I saved yours too, so we're even," I said dryly.

He shrugged with one shoulder and winced. Apparently his arm still hurt after all.

"What about the rest of you?" I asked. My gaze swung up to Nash, who seemed angry, for some inexplicable reason.

"I knew, but only after we—" he hesitated, "got involved."

Matt shot him a look of surprise, then made a face as if disgusted that anyone might be interested in me.

Yeah, fuck you too, I thought.

"How much after?" I asked.

"After you got that tattoo," Nash said. "I spoke to Matt about it. He told me about your mother and Ariana."

My heart sank deeper. Even if they were trying to

protect me, they had kept so many secrets from me, I wasn't sure I could trust them.

"No one thought to ask me what I thought about any of this?" I growled.

"I didn't know anything about it," Kane assured me.

"Neither did I," Dyson said quickly. "You saw what Peyton did out there today? All the rest of us could do was to stand there and watch. She's more badass than we are."

"Exactly," Kane agreed. "She can take care of herself."

"Thank you," I told them both.

"If you think that, you're all fools," Matt said derisively. "That was one phoenix. One attack. What will they send next time? People with guns? An army of dragons?" He jerked his chin toward Nash. "Now they know the academy is here, they'll come after us all. This is now about more than Peyton. Every student here is at risk."

"Then we'll move the academy," Nash said. "It wouldn't be the first time."

I blew a breath out pursed lips. "So them coming after me has revealed the existence of the academy? All because of my mother. Why not go after her? Why kill me?"

"It's unlikely they want to kill you," Nash said. His tone gave me chills.

Oh yeah, that whole making paranormal babies against my will thing, I had forgotten about that.

Matt nodded his agreement. "At best they might hold you until your mother complies with their wishes. At worst, they'll break you until you beg to help them."

"Fuck no," I muttered.

"We're not going to let anything happen to you," Kane assured me.

"Me either," Dyson said. "We can pack up and leave right now if you want to. We can go somewhere far away, where they can't find us."

That was tempting.

I sighed. "If we do that, we'll spend the rest of our lives looking over our shoulders."

"We all do that already," Matt pointed out. "More so now they know we're here. Every minute we delay, gives them time to rally and come after us."

"I should have killed the phoenix when I had the chance." Nash scowled.

"Why didn't you?" Matt turned accusing eyes toward him.

Nash gave him a dark look, but I knew what he was thinking. The lives he had taken haunted him as it was. He didn't want to add to that body count. Not to mention Zeta would find him if he shifted into dragon form. They would know where he'd hidden and come after him, hard.

"It's done now," I said softly. "We need to deal with today and tomorrow."

"Peyton," Ariana started.

"I don't want to hear it," I snapped.

She flinched as if I'd struck her. "I was only trying to—"

I cut her off. "You pretended to be my friend. I cared about you, but you were lying to me the whole time!"

Tears spilled down her cheeks. "I was your friend." She sniffed. "I *am* your friend. Just because I was sent to help, doesn't mean I didn't care."

I shook my head. "You should have told me." I glanced toward Nash. "You too."

His mouth twitched downward. "I told you what I could. I was scared you'd risk yourself if you knew any more." His eyes were full of regret, but I forced myself to look away.

"And you." I jerked my head toward Matt. "That was you that day with Jess."

"Yep," he replied easily. "I thought I'd check you out, see what you're made of."

"That earth shake," I said, "that was you?"

"I might have rocked your world a little bit." He didn't even look slightly sorry for it.

"People could have died," I reminded him.

He rolled his eyes. "Everyone was fine. I know how to be careful."

"Sure you do." I pointed toward his arm. "How's that going?"

He pulled his sleeve up to reveal skin covered in nasty scars. "I'll have a nice reminder of how I tried to save the ass of an ungrateful brat."

I bared my teeth at him. "Who are you—"

"Enough," Nash snapped. "We fucked up. We should have been honest with you, but we don't have time for you to be butt hurt."

I gaped at him. Butt hurt? Because my best friend and my lover had been lying to me? I was more than butt hurt, I was furious, and with good reason. A little voice in the back of my head reminded me they had just been trying to keep me safe, but I was too angry to pay it much attention.

"Everyone go and pack, but lightly. We need to evacuate the building as soon as possible." Nash waved us toward the door.

Kane gripped my hand. "I'll help you."

I regarded him for a moment. "You worked with Nash. He really said nothing about any of this?"

Kane licked his lips. "Uh."

"What the fuck, Kane?" Dyson snapped.

What the fuck indeed.

"It's not like that," Kane protested. "He just suggested I be careful if we go anywhere. And…look out for anyone who might follow us."

"Did you ask why?" Dyson asked.

Kane's mouth worked for a moment. "Not really, no. I agreed to be careful and that was that."

There was more to this, but we didn't have time for that right now.

I pulled my hand from his and stood. "I can pack my own bags. You all worry about yours."

Kane shot me look of pure hurt and got to his feet. "If I'd known, I would have told you."

"You didn't tell me Nash gave you that warning," I said curtly.

"No, but—"

"Then don't say you would have, because you didn't," I snapped. "I can't trust a single one of you."

Dyson raised a finger. "I swear, I knew nothing about any of this."

"I told you about Nash's warning," Kane said softly.

He might as well have reached into my chest and pulled out my beating heart. Hot tears pooled in my eyes and trickled down my cheeks. I put up my hands before anyone could say another word.

"I'm done with all of you." I swallowed to hold back a sob. I felt as though my whole life lay in ruins around my feet, like they'd stomped all over it. "I'm going to pack and when I'm done, I never want to see any of you, ever again."

"You don't mean that," Ariana said. She reached a hand out to me.

"I mean every word," I assured her. At the time I did. Later, when I had calmed down, I might think differently. Right now though, I felt sick and wanted to be away from these people. "Stay the hells away from me."

"Peyton—"

I didn't know who spoke, I had already turned my back and hurried out the door. Once there, I broke into a trot, pushed past other students and ignored the one or two people who asked if I was okay.

It wasn't until I was alone in my room that I broke down into sobs. How had my perfect little piece of the world come to this? I had never felt so alone, so betrayed, in my entire life.

I pulled my bag out from under my bed and threw things inside it. I didn't know what most of it was, I was looking through a haze of tears. Maybe I should leave it all here and get away from the academy. And maybe a part of me needed to take the time to pack, in the hope one of my friends or lovers came with words that would heal my heart. Or start to.

23

THE KNOCK on the door told me it wasn't Ariana. As strained as things were between us, she would have just unlocked the door and come in.

At first I didn't bother to answer it. I zipped up my suitcase and pulled it to the floor by the handle.

Whoever it was, knocked again. Harder this time.

I sighed and opened the door.

"If I was a Zeta agent, you'd be dead or in captivity," Matt said.

I groaned. "Why did they send you?" Of all people.

He pushed the door open further and stepped inside. On his back, he wore a backpack which was almost as big as I was.

"Because I'm the only one who is going to give it

to you straight and not try to spare your feelings." He fixed me with a firm look.

I crossed my arms over my chest. "Go on then."

"You're overreacting and being a brat," he declared.

"Okay. You've told me, now you can leave." I tugged my suitcase toward the door.

Matt made a frustrated sound in the back of his throat. He placed a hand on the doorframe. I could get past, but I'd have to duck.

"Everything everyone has done for you was to keep you safe. What would you have said if they had explained everything earlier? Be honest. With yourself, if not with me."

I frowned. "I would have been pissed off. I don't need babysitting."

"If that phoenix had attacked while you were out jogging, what would you have done?" he asked. "If I hadn't been there today, you would have been taken. Right there, in front of the academy. And no one could have stopped them. By now, you'd be so broken you'd be telling them every detail about this place."

"Fuck off, I would not," I snapped.

I caught a hint of a smile. He was trying to goad me. Asshole. It had worked.

"All right, maybe in an hour or two. The point is, you needed help and you wouldn't have accepted it if you'd known we were offering it. Admit it."

I opened my mouth to protest but sighed instead. "Fine. You're right, I wouldn't have wanted it." I would probably have gone off by myself to prove what a badass I was.

He smirked. "Did you just say I'm right? I should have recorded that, I bet you don't say it often."

I rolled my eyes. "Yeah, yeah, don't let it go to your head."

"Which one?" he shot back.

"The one on your shoulders," I said firmly. "I have no interest in the one in your pants."

"That's only because you've never tried it." He grinned. "Believe me, I could have you screaming for hours."

"Says you." I stepped closer to the door, which meant closer to him. He did smell good, like soap and testosterone. "Shouldn't we be evacuating?"

"After you promise to speak to your friends. Ariana in particular is beside herself. Kane too. When I left, he looked like he was about to cry." Matt lowered his arm and stepped back.

"Not that there's anything wrong with men crying," I said sternly.

"If you say so." He grabbed the handle of my suit-case from my hand and pulled it down the corridor.

"What, too much of a big man to show emotion?" I asked teasingly.

"No, I don't waste my time with crying over people and stuff." He stopped to push the button beside the elevator.

"That's actually really sad," I told him. "What about things like love?"

"No time for that either." The elevator doors slide open and he pulled my suitcase in, in front of me.

"Or basic manners," I muttered.

"What? I'm pulling your suitcase, aren't I?" He pushed the button for the ground floor.

"So we'll move faster, not because you're nice."

"True," he agreed.

The elevator started down with a jolt.

"Where are the others?" I asked.

Before he could respond, the elevator jerked to a stop and the lights went out.

"Oh crap," he murmured.

"Let me guess, that's not a coincidence." I leaned against the wall and rubbed my face.

"It's highly unlikely to be one, yes," he agreed. "We're going to need to get out of—"

From outside the elevator an enormous bang

sounded. The floor shook so hard I was thrown off my feet. I hit the wall with a thud and cried out in pain.

"Shit." A ball of magic lit Matt's face. He held out his palm to illuminate me. "Are you okay?"

"Yeah." I pulled myself to my feet. "It's just my dignity that's bruised."

"Good. As I was saying, we need to get out of here," he said. "Can you open the door?"

I nodded and reached for my phone. I knew just the spell. We'd been working on it in class.

"Uh, fuckity-crap," I swore. My phone screen must had been smashed when I fell. It flared for a moment, then what looked like a trickle of magic rose from the broken screen. It hovered in the air in front of my face for a moment, then shot up through the elevator roof and was gone.

"Just when you think things can't get worse," I growled.

"That was a—" Matt pointed upward, his mouth agape.

"I know what it was," I told him. "It's a tracking spell. The question is, why was it there?" I groaned inwardly. That must have been what was causing havoc with my phone, and why Zeta knew where to look. Why hadn't Madame Luc recognised it?

"Actually, the question is how long will it take before Zeta finds us here now that spell has broadcast your presence to any paranormal who knows to look for it?" He rubbed his face and shook his head. "There's no point in being subtle now. We can just blast the door open." He raised his hand.

"Wait." I grabbed his arm. "There might be people out there. You could kill someone."

"Right." Beads of sweat coated his brow.

"Claustrophobic?" I guessed.

"Yeah." He swallowed audibly.

"In that case—"

Something thudded onto the roof and the elevator jolted. Whatever it was started to scratch just above our heads.

Matt's face paled.

I squeezed his arm. "We'll get out of here, don't worry." I tried to sound reassuring, but the scratching increased. "Maybe I should blast that?" I pointed upward.

Before Matt could respond, the maintenance hatch above our heads moved. We shrank back into a corner. I know, it was pointless trying to hide in a space so small I could touch either wall with my arms outstretched. Instinct is what it is.

The hatch slid aside to reveal Dyson's smiling face. "Hey strangers. You look like you need a hand."

"Are you naked?" I asked without thinking. Fear does strange things to people's minds. In my case in particular.

He grinned. "I had to shift to get down here. Sorry I don't have a change of clothes stored on top of an elevator."

"Of course," I muttered. "You should help Matt out first. He looks like he's about to pass out."

Matt shot me a dirty look and drew himself up taller. "I'm fine."

"Sure you are," I said dryly. "Now is not the time to pull that macho shit. Get up there. You can help pull me out afterward."

Dyson lay on his stomach and offered Matt his hand.

"I don't need help," Matt grunted. He pulled off his clothes and tossed them to me.

I caught them and held them in front of me, high enough to give him some privacy. Okay, I did peek and ye gads, he was big. I mean, *huge*. My mouth went dry at the thought of him sliding into... Ugh, that was Matt I was thinking about. I reminded myself I couldn't stand him and looked away.

I glanced back in time to see him shift into his

gargoyle form. Up close, he was impressive. Rippling muscles and midnight dark hide. His back legs bunched under him and he leapt just as Dyson moved out of the way.

In one leap he was atop the elevator and shifted back into human form.

"Here." I threw his clothes up toward him. He caught them and moved out of sight. Judging by the way the elevator moved, he was getting dressed.

Priorities.

I rolled my eyes and pulled my suitcase under the hatch so I could climb up onto it. Hopefully the hard plastic would support my weight.

"We heard an explosion," I said when Dyson reappeared above me.

He looked over at something beside him and grimaced. "Yeah. We need to hurry up. Things are getting—"

The elevator jolted again and I was thrown off my suitcase and hard against the wall. Pain blossomed through my shoulder and down to the rest of my arm.

"Peyton!" Dyson called out. "I don't think this thing is going to hold much longer."

"Get yourselves to safety," I shouted back. Tears

poured down my cheeks. I didn't think my arm was broken, but it sure hurt like hells.

"We're not leaving without—shit!"

The whole elevator shook like we were inside a snow globe. I was tossed against one wall, then the other. Just as I decided I would probably die here, the elevator car went completely still.

"Matt's holding it," Dyson said. "Come on!"

Wincing, I pulled my suitcase back into place and climbed onto it again.

The elevator gave an ominous creak.

"This is why you should take stairs during an emergency," I said under my breath.

Teetering on top of the suitcase, I put my hand up above my head. It took two tries before Dyson was able to grab hold.

With a grunt, he pulled me up though the hatch. I flopped down beside him to catch my breath.

Matt stood an arm span away, half dressed, a look of concentration on his face. Magic danced around him like an aura. "Hurry up," he growled.

"We'll have to climb up to the next level." Dyson gestured.

I followed the direction he pointed. We were a couple of metres down. The cables that should have held us were frayed as if they'd been hacked. If Matt faltered…

"You go first," I told Dyson. "I'm guessing your dog form can jump that distance."

He nodded. "Unless you can conjure a ladder."

"If my phone wasn't smashed, I'd try that," I assured him.

He looked regretful. "Mine is with my clothes. Matt?"

"What?" Matt grunted.

"Do you have your phone with you?" Dyson asked.

"It's in my jeans pocket," he replied.

Since he wasn't wearing any jeans, I crawled over to the pile of clothes near his feet. I searched his pockets and pulled out his phone.

"Passcode." I glanced toward him.

"Six, nine, six, nine," he said.

"Of course it is," I muttered. I pressed in the code and opened the browser. Either he didn't search up anything, or he'd cleaned his history recently. I tapped in the website we'd used in class and scrolled down to the advanced lessons. Yes, conjuring creatures is a basic skill, go figure.

I found a selection of objects and clicked on the link. "Boxes, tables, chairs…"

"Hurry up," Matt urged.

"I'm trying," I replied. "Why the fuck would I conjure a temporary waterslide?" I shook my head. "Ah, there was go. Ladder." I clicked and focused on the floor between my feet and the level above us.

After a moment, a ladder shimmered into existence.

"Perfect." I tucked the phone into my pocket.

"Ladies first." Dyson gave me a bow.

I don't know about lady, but I was the one who couldn't shift and get myself out, so I grabbed the ladder and climbed up and out of the shaft.

Grateful, I flopped down onto the carpet and took a few breaths.

Before I could even move out of the way to let Dyson up, footsteps approached.

"We've found her!"

The words were followed by a snap and the sound of the elevator dropping to the floor below.

2 4

<hr>

I ROLLED over and jumped to my feet. My first instinct was to run back to the elevator shaft and make sure the guys were all right. Instead, I froze. I had other things to deal with first.

What I assumed were Zeta agents stood with guns trained on me. They were both dressed from head to toe in black. Total cliché, am I right? Black is such a badass colour, it didn't deserve to be appropriated by an evil organisation. They should wear a hideous colour, like muddy brown or olive green. Maybe a nice orange.

I eyed their guns. "Hey guys. Nice of you to come and help."

"Hands up." The agent on the left—a guy with a butt-chin—gestured with his weapon.

In spite of the pain in my arm, I raised my hands slowly but kept my gaze on them and their weapons. I wasn't used to dealing with guns, but I figured if they were going to fire, I would see it in their movements before they pulled the trigger.

"Turn around and walk toward the stairs." Butt-chin ordered.

I considered for a moment. On one hand, I didn't want to have my back to them. That would put me at a distinct disadvantage. On the other hand, Matt said they didn't want me dead. If they knew who I was, I was better off going along with them until the right moment came to fight back.

"Now," the other agent growled. She had a twitch in one eye that gave away her nerves.

I turned slowly and started to walk.

From other parts of the academy the sound of shouting echoed. Every now and again, someone would scream, or a crash would resound. The floor shook under my feet. That couldn't be good.

"Faster." Twitchy-eye poked a gun in my back.

"Hey, I'm going as fast as I can," I replied. The smart ass in me was tempted to slow down, but instinct to survive overrode that. I didn't want to die if the building collapsed and I didn't want to get shot. What I did want was to be sure Dyson was all right. Okay, maybe I was a bit worried about Matt too. Who would I argue with if he was gone?

I chewed my lip. Where the hells were Nash, Kane and Ariana? I wished I hadn't wasted so much time being angry with them. It seemed so silly now. All they had been trying to do was save me from… well…this exact situation. Here I was anyway. Just great.

Hopefully they all got out and ran. Knowing them, they stayed to look for me, but I hoped they had more sense. Firstly, I didn't feel I deserved to have them risk themselves more than they already had, and secondly it wouldn't help anyone if they got killed. Or taken.

I stepped around a corner and found the first of the bodies. One looked to be a student I didn't recognise. The other was a Zeta agent, a frozen look of fear on their face. Score one for our team. And one for theirs.

I shuffled around them and down the first few stairs. Here, there were another two bodies. Another Zeta agent and… I swallowed hard.

Madame Luc.

If the gaping hole in her chest was anything to go by, she'd been shot. The Zeta agent was missing a large amount of their face, so I guessed she won that round.

At the bottom of the stairs, the shouting escalated. If I had to guess, I would say Zeta had us outnumbered. The only way to take on a bunch of witches, wizards, shifters and hybrids would be to do it with strength of numbers. Anything else would be suicide. Unless they had a lot of hybrids on their side. I couldn't discount that possibility.

"Down the next set of stairs," Butt-chin ordered.

"I think that would be a bad idea," I said. "It sounds like people are dying down there. Would it be better to, I don't know, hide for a while?"

"Walk," Twitchy-eye snapped. She jabbed me with her gun again.

"If I fall and break my neck, you're going to get into trouble," I pointed out. "Whoever or whatever your boss is, they want me alive."

"Quiet," Butt-chin said. "Move."

"Charming," I said under my breath. I walked, but as I did, I drew back my sleeve, under the pretence of scratching an itch. I licked my lips and waited.

Five steps.

Four steps.

Three steps.

Two steps.

I turned and conjured the gargoyle. As soon as it appeared, I threw myself through the door at the bottom of the stairs and slammed it shut behind me.

The ear-piercing scream that followed wasn't even slightly satisfying. I took no pleasure in hurting or killing anyone, even if they would happily kill me first.

I ran from the stairs to the elevator just as the doors were blasted outward. I threw a hand over my eyes to shield them from flying shards of metal.

"Peyton, there you are!" Dyson said cheerfully.

I lowered my hand to see him stand in the remains of the doorway in all his naked glory. He caught me up in a big embrace.

Matt, still half-naked, was right behind him.

"You're all right?" I asked once Dyson loosened his hold on me. I fixed my gaze on his and drank in the warm, tender look in his eyes.

"More or less," Matt replied. "Thanks for caring."

I stuck my tongue out at him. "I'm glad you're okay too," I told him, "even if you are a pain in the ass."

"Back at you," he said gruffly. Maybe he didn't hate me after all.

"Fuck." Dyson's eyes widened. He cocked his head like a dog listening to something.

"What is it?" I asked.

The doors to the stairs burst open and a creature leapt out. Head of an eagle, body of a lion, twitching eye, the griffin looked pissed off. Claw marks ran down the side of her face. Butt-chin lay near her feet, or at least his head did.

Two points to the gargoyle. Or maybe one and a half, since Twitchy-eye was still around.

She thrust her head forward and made a strange, low cry.

"I hate griffins," Matt muttered.

"I think the feeling is mutual," Dyson said.

She stalked toward us.

I reassessed the danger to the academy. The numbers of Zeta agents might not be as high as I assumed, but if they had enough hybrids like this, we might be in trouble.

"What can we use against her?" I stepped back until the wall was right behind me.

The griffin licked her lips. Of course, she could understand every word. She seemed to be enjoying this. I guessed in her normal form, she didn't get as much respect as she did as a griffin.

"Maybe her insecurity," I suggested. I stepped toward her. "Hey, there's no reason we should be on opposite sides. We're all paranormals here. We could be—"

She lunged at me and swung an enormous paw.

Only instinct let me duck aside in time for the swing to pass over my head close enough to slice off a few hairs.

"Opposite sides it is then," I said under my breath. I fired a ball of magic and threw it while I rolled out of the way and back on my feet.

She hissed, but formed a bubble fast enough to deflect the worst of my magic.

"Peyton." Dyson grabbed my hand and tugged me toward the door leading out of the academy.

I made a bubble around us both, in case she threw any magic back at me. What we gained in invisibility, we lost with the noise we made as we ran across the tiled floor.

"Ouch!"

A voice cried out at the same time as I stepped something soft. "Sorry." Apparently we weren't the only invisible ones making a run for it out of here. No doubt whoever's foot I stepped on would be okay.

We ran out to the road, Matt behind us.

The road was filled with discarded items left by

students who had fled the Zeta attack. Several agents lay dead or dying.

Dyson pulled me down behind a car and Matt crouched on the other side.

"This is why they want hybrids?" I guessed. "They're bloody hard to kill."

"Let's hope some of us are," Matt said.

The griffin ran past us, then stopped and turned back. She cocked her head and stuck out a pointed tongue as though to taste the air. Or our fear.

"I need a distraction," Matt whispered.

I nodded and I pulled his phone out of my pocket. I tapped on the screen, grimaced as I entered the passcode and clicked on our magical website.

"No offence, but maybe a bit faster," Dyson said, "she looks like she wants to bite off my dick."

"Well, we can't have that," I said without looking up. I found what I was looking for and clicked.

A magpie appeared in the air above the griffin. The little black and white bird let out a squawk and dove at the griffin. It managed to deliver a series of pecks to the griffin's head before she swatted it away.

It was enough to allow Matt to shift and throw himself at her. He fastened his great jaw on her neck.

His claws gripped her body until blood coated his front feet.

In spite of that, the griffin only shook her head and batted at Matt with her huge claws. They raked down his skin, drawing shining blood on his black hide.

"Matt!" I stood and tossed a ball of magic at her, then another. They struck her, but she had a bubble up before I could blink.

"Fuck, she's fast." I crouched back down.

"Stay here." A moment later, Dyson was in his dog form. He jumped toward the griffin. He was a wolfhound, I realised. Big, shaggy and apparently nasty when they're pissed. He grabbed hold of one of the griffin's legs with his teeth and growled.

She shook her leg to try to shake him off, but he held on fast.

"Good dog," I muttered.

The griffin loosened her grip on Matt and he fell to the ground with a thud. Blood seeped from his wounds and spread across the road.

"Gods." I swallowed hard. I wanted to run out there and drag him to safety. Even as I thought that, he groaned, lifted his head and shifted. Naked, he forced himself to his knees and crawled toward me.

His back was marred with gouges, but they were already starting to heal.

The griffin screeched, then screeched again. She shook her leg so hard I thought Dyson might fly off, but he stayed attached.

A new sound reached my ears—a low growl and the sound of wings. Very large wings. A shadow passed overhead.

I licked my lips and looked up as the body of a dragon flew over the top of the car and over us. He swooped down toward the griffin, who looked terrified for the first time.

She turned and attempted to run, but Dyson's weight held her back.

The dragon opened his mouth. Huge teeth shone in the afternoon sun like a set of knives. He huffed out a breath of what looked like magic. That was even more badass than breathing fire.

When Nash was close enough, he leaned down and bit off the griffin's head. Blood squirted from her neck and onto his muzzle and the street around her.

Her body teetered for a moment, then fell.

Dyson just managed to let go and leap out of the way before she crashed to the road.

"And that's how you kill a hybrid," Matt said wearily.

"That's good to know," I muttered, before I leaned over and threw up my breakfast on the ground beside me.

25

THE STREET WAS QUIET NOW. The residents who had peeked out of their homes had all been reassured they'd witnessed nothing more than filming for some Hollywood blockbuster. Later maybe someone would realise they would have had to sign release forms and vacate the premises while filming was going on. Then there was the lack of cameras. By the time they figured any of that out, we would be long gone, along with anything they'd filmed on their own phones.

All of that was left to the teachers and administrators. The students who weren't dead or evacuated already, huddled together near the front doors.

"I'll organise the bus for the rest of us," Nash had said before he'd hurried away to do his teacherly stuff and find some clothes. Matt and Dyson had found shirts and underwear, neither of which fit well, but at least they weren't naked. Not that I minded, but they looked uncomfortable walking around outside like that. And let's face it, there was much more chance of having a dick bitten off when it was uncovered.

I leaned against Kane, who sat with his arm around me. Ariana sat on my other side, her face pale.

"So what happened to you two?" I asked.

Kane looked embarrassed. "We got trapped on the third floor when the elevator stopped working. We hid until it was safe to take the stairs."

"Oh, that's good," I said awkwardly. "Um, I mean I'm glad you're both okay." So what if they hadn't fought? They'd done well to stay clear of trouble.

Ariana turned to me, her eyes bright with tears. "Really? I'm so sorry I lied to you. I was...I was..." She sniffed.

I patted her shoulder. "You were trying to keep me safe. I get it now. I'm sorry I was a bitch."

Kane gave me a squeeze. "You're allowed to be angry. No one would blame you. And you were never a bitch."

"Yes I was," I said. "I blame me." I sighed through

my nose. I had gone off half cocked and that could have gotten us all killed. I wouldn't have forgiven myself if anything bad had happened. Well, anything worse than what already had.

I looked from one to the other, then at Matt and Dyson. "Can we agree from now on, to keep each other safe, and to be honest about everything?"

"I agree." Dyson sat near my feet, wearing an oversized purple t-shirt with a fairy on it. It looked more like a nightgown than a shirt, but he was adorable in it.

"I agree," Ariana said softly.

"Me three," Kane agreed.

We all looked toward Matt, whose shirt was lime green. I had no idea who he'd borrowed it from, but it suited him. For a guy who loathed me, he was pretty cute.

"What? I was always honest with you." He shrugged. "Besides, we don't like each other, remember?" He gave me a look which suggested otherwise.

For some silly reason, my heart did a little flip. Gods, as if I wasn't busy enough with Kane, Dyson and Nash. Still, I wondered what it would feel like to run my hands down his abs, to take his cock…

I cleared my throat. "You didn't tell me you were following me, when you started doing it."

"What kind of secret agent would I be if I revealed myself to you like that?" he asked. A smile tugged at the corners of his mouth.

"Is that what you are?" I asked. "A secret agent?"

"What else?" He raised an eyebrow at me. "We're supposed to be secret, but some of us are already working against Zeta." He nodded toward Ariana.

"I think we all have a score to settle," Dyson said, as if he was talking about the weather.

"I'm not sure if this was what I signed up for," I said carefully.

"It doesn't seem like Zeta gave you a choice," Ariana pointed out.

"They'll come again," Matt said darkly.

"When?" I bit my lip.

"It could be days, it could be decades." Matt shrugged. "In the meantime, they'll find us a place to study which should be safe."

"*Should*," I echoed. "That's the keyword there."

"While paranormals exist outside their control, they'll be looking for us. They won't like having so many of us off their leash."

My tongue darted over my lips. "I'd rather die than take part in whatever they have planned."

"You might get that option," Matt said.

"That's a cheerful thought." I nestled down deeper in Kane's arms. He gave me a kiss on my cheek.

"We won't let that happen," he assured me. "To you, or to anyone."

"Yeah, what Kane said," Dyson agreed. "We'll take care of each other, like a little family. Ariana is the little sister, Nash is the uncle who isn't related to any of us by blood. And Matt is…"

Matt shot him a look. "What is Matt?"

"You're that cousin who pretends he's too cool for the rest of us, but is really just as much of a geek," I told him.

He snorted and shook his head but didn't seem to mind the assessment. "For the record, I *am* that cool."

I laughed, but it faded when Nash stepped out of the academy doors. He looked exhausted and haunted. It didn't take magic to know he was thinking about the griffin he'd killed. The fact he'd had no choice didn't mean it wouldn't trouble him, probably forever.

"The bus will be here soon," he said. "They'll take us to a safe location where we can all rest. They'll decide what to do with us after that."

The fact he included himself made my heart sing. At least, as much as it could on such a heavy day.

"At least we got final exams out of the way," Dyson said.

"Very thoughtful of them," Kane said ironically.

Nash forced a faint smile and turned at the sound of an approaching engine.

A long bus drew to a stop outside the academy and a large man with arms covered in tattoos climbed out of the driver's seat.

"Dick!" he said loudly.

Nash scowled at him. "It's Nash to you, Johnny."

Johnny grinned. "Oh yeah. Well, whatever. Rob and Marion send their regards. Rob's found a place to stash you all for a while."

I found myself smiling at the man. He seemed like the kind of guy people adored on sight. Not like a lover, but as a friend and ally.

"Thanks Johnny." Nash gave him a curt nod and gestured toward us. "Everyone on before they wonder what happened to the attackers and come looking."

From what I could gather, fifty Zeta agents had come against us. As well as the griffin, they'd had two more hybrids. The academy's own hybrids had teamed up to behead them as Nash had done. Well—with claws and a sword, rather than teeth. I reminded myself to have a sword tattooed on my arm the moment we found time. I never knew when that might be useful.

We held back until the rest of the students climbed aboard. Some of them looked in worse shape than we were. One had gashes down her cheek. Another was covered in blood, but I didn't know if it was theirs or someone else's.

Ariana climbed the stairs into the bus ahead of me. Before I could take a step up, Nash grabbed my hand and pulled me to him. He pressed his mouth down hard on mine. He thrust his tongue into my mouth, withdrew it and ran it across my lips.

Just as my knees went weak, he pulled back and gave me a push toward the bus. "Hurry up," he growled.

I snorted at him but licked my lips in what I hoped was a provocative way.

He gave me a look that clearly said the moment we were alone, he was going to tear off my clothes and fuck me senseless. That was fine by me.

Johnny grinned and gave me a wink.

I blushed, grabbed the handrail and climbed up into the bus. Kane, Dyson and Matt followed close behind.

We all tumbled into seats near the back of the bus. Kane and I shared a seat. Dyson and Matt shared the seat behind us. Ariana sat in front, with Violette.

"Hey look, someone even thought to give us blankets," Kane said. He waited until we were seated and draped one over us both. He drew me closer and draped his arms around me. With the blanket covering us, no one could see him slip a hand inside my shirt to caress my nipple.

I gulped.

The bus door closed and we pulled away from the academy. From the outside, it didn't look like it had been a war zone recently. Even the street looked like a place of relative calm in a big city.

"So much for the Academy of Modern Magic," I sighed.

"We're still academy students," Kane replied. "We're just moving to a new campus, that's all." He leaned in to nibble my earlobe. "I'm glad you're okay," he whispered. He rolled my nipple between his thumb and forefinger. His other hand slipped down between my legs.

"Me too," I replied. I parted my legs and let him rub lightly at the front of my jeans.

"I've never met anyone like you." He undid the button of my jeans and tugged the zipper open.

"I could say the same about you." I lifted my hips

for long enough for him to push my jeans down my hips.

"I want you to choose me," he said softly. He pulled my panties aside and dipped his fingers down to my entrance.

Oh, that whole choosing thing. The problem was, I didn't want to have to choose. I liked Kane, Dyson and Nash equally. They all drove me wild and made me hot as hells. Even Matt wasn't without his charm.

Kane slid his fingers inside me and rubbed my clit with the back of his hand. With the other, he pulled down the blanket and my shirt to expose my breasts. If the guys behind us peeked in between the seats, they would get a nice little show. For some reason, that made me more aroused than ever.

I glanced back and caught a sign of movement, but I couldn't tell which guy moved or if they were watching. For some reason, my imagination conjured Matt, his hand under the blanket of his lap, fingers wound around his cock, his grip sliding up and down as he pleasured himself while he watched. The thought made my mouth drier than ever. Gods, what these guys all did to me.

I bit back a moan and bucked against Kane's hand. He rubbed harder while his fingertips toyed with my nipples.

My imagination pictured Dyson's mouth on my hard peaks, suckling and licking, running his tongue over my breasts. Beside him, Matt pumped harder until Nash appeared and took his cock into his mouth. Holy fuck, where did *that* come from, and was it wrong that I wanted to see that in real life?

I gritted my teeth to hold back a moan as I came, hard and intense. Pleasure flooded me, wiping out all thoughts of our horrible day, at least for a while. It washed away any thoughts of moving to a new campus and having to choose a lover.

When I came down, I would think about that. For now, I would let myself be lost in the moment, the excitement of being alive and having three incredible guys who seemed to like me as much as I liked them. We had defeated Zeta and passed our final exams.

Second year would be very different, but we had each other. That would get us through anything.

Let them come.

We'll be ready.

EPILOGUE

OUTSIDE THE HOUSE was dark and still. I stopped to glance out the window. In spite of the relative peace of the last few weeks, I was still jumpy. I took a deep breath in and told myself to calm. I was safe here, in my parent's house. I was—

A shadow crossed in front of the moon.

Shit.

I froze. Whatever it was, it was big. *Really* big.

It banked and passed in front of the moon again, then out of sight.

I stood and waited, my breath caught in my throat.

The only thing which broke the silence was the wind and my racing heart. I strained to see, but the night was still again. Nothing moved but the leaves on the trees.

That didn't help me shake the feeling something was out there waiting.

Waiting for me.

WILL PEYTON CHOOSE? Will Zeta catch her? Who has the bigger dick, a dragon or a gargoyle? To find out, read on with Virtual Magic.

ABOUT THE AUTHOR

Maggie Alabaster is the reverse harem and fantasy romance pen name of author Mirren Hogan.

She lives in NSW, Australia with one spouse, two daughters, dog, cat, rabbits and countless birds.

Sign up for my newsletter! Sign Up!

Join my reader group! Join here!

Follow me on Bookbub! Click here to follow me!

Summer's Harem

Book 1: Shimmer

Book 2: Glimmer

Book 3: Flicker

Complete collection

Short reads

Taken by the Snowmen

Jingle All the Way

Also by Maggie Alabaster and Erin Yoshikawa

Caught by the Tide

Book 1–Pursued by Shadows

Book 2 Pursued by Darkness

Book 3 Pursued by Monsters